My Name is Maysel

Best Wishes to Donna, one of
my most highly respected
friends.

[signature]

2010

Enjoy!

Published by American Imaging
(www.ebookproducers.com)

Cover design: Jim Grich
Format and packaging: Peggy Grich
Photography: Angela Fellenz (843-281-8484)

Printed in the United States of America

ISBN: 978-1-61539-773-0

This book is based on actual characters. Some names have been changed to protect the privacy of the individuals involved.

My Name is Maysel

by

Johnny McCarty

DEDICATED TO THE MEMORY
OF

Wannie and Maysel McCarty
and
Jack and Lela Trout

My Name is Maysel

Chapter 1

The sun was shining on the delicate, 17-year-old face of Lela Pittsenbarger as she walked up the narrow path towards her home. Its warmth felt good after spending a long cold winter in the hills of rural West Virginia. If the world didn't know depression, sacrifice, and doing without, they surely could get a good dose of it here. Houses were not located close to each other, the area was sparsely populated, but those who lived around Lela tried to look after each other. Living with her mother and father was not a bad thing; it was just that the only abundant thing in her life was God and love.

Finding work enough to support a wife and teen-aged daughter in the year 1921 was not an easy thing to do. Laboring in the fields of more-fortunate people all day long would provide just enough food to last a few days. Sometimes, a very lucky person would earn money, instead of the usual trade of labor for food. Today it may be potatoes, tomorrow may be tomatoes, and the next day's payment just might be green beans. Yes, every day, her father had to trust in God and pray for good health to survive. Oh well, at least she wasn't hungry, and for that she was grateful.

She knew lots of folks in this countryside community who were. It made her heart sad to think of the many people who lived without enough food and needed shelter.

"Lela!" She heard her mother's voice call to her as she was brought back from her reverie. Thoughts of what her life would hold sooner or later. She often dreamed of a nice God-fearing, hard-working, loving husband to be the father of her children. She longed for a warm, safe place for her future family to live in peace and love. Love . . . a very important ingredient in the recipe for marriage. She guessed these thoughts were normal for all 17-year-old girls. "I hope God doesn't mind my dreaming," she thought. Dreams of love and family were really all there was to hold on to in these most depressing times. After all, her faith in Him was absolutely unshakable.

"Lela! Do you hear me? Her mother yelled.

"Yes Mama. I'll be right there!" Having Mama to wait was not a good thing. She was very much a disciplinarian and Lela did not want to provoke her. "It'll soon be time for supper, and then we have to go to church." Church was a big part of their lives. This family never missed a service. Rain or shine, if no one else was there . . . they were. Her mother told her, "I'm glad there's no more school for you this year. We won't have to get up early tomorrow. Get cleaned up a little. You know how your father dislikes slouchy girls." Lela was his only child and at the end of each workday, he expected the "apple of his eye" to be picture-perfect. She always was. As far as she was concerned, her father was everything any man should want to be, and everything any woman would ever want in a man. Her heart's desire was to someday meet and marry a man much like him.

Spring announced itself loud and clear with vivid yellow forsythia, daffodils, and other early spring flowers. Her parents always liked the ground (small as the house and grounds were) to look as pretty as possible. The fact that they were not rich didn't necessarily mean that their place had to be ugly, and look unattended. All the flowers were a welcomed sight for Lela. Seeing them let her know for certain that spring was here and that there would be activities around the church, which just might render her a beau.

Stepping inside the house, she could smell the wonderful fragrant bouquet of her mother's cooking. She could always feel her mother's love. Mama always worked hard making certain that Lela lacked very little of the necessities of life, even if she had to do without things herself. If it be a kind hug and kiss of appreciation for something Lela had done, or a necessary act of correction for some small error, Lela felt secure in knowing that both of her parents loved her more than anything on earth.

Nina Pittsenbarger looked up from her work to see her daughter come through the front door of their small home. Ah! There it was. That rush! Nothing thrilled her more than to look at Lela and feel the familiar wave of pride, love and admiration that flooded through her every time she did. Lela was an honorable, young, pretty thing. Not too tall, about five foot one, and weighing about 115 pounds, she was a picture to look at. Lela was as sweet as honey, innocent as a newborn, and as dependable as the sun that rises each morning. Perfect? Maybe. Lela had given her parents absolutely no problems. Nina was proud to have given birth to this wonderful girl and even more so when she looked at her own reflection in the mirror, and could see the similarities between herself and Lela. Lela looked remarkably like her mother. The long heavy hair which both of them kept tied in a full ponytail, their big, bright blue eyes, even their posture was the same. Their likes and dislikes in food, their habits, everything was so much alike. They could be sisters were it not for the number of years between their ages. Yes, it looked as though Nina had been cloned and it gave the older one great joy when people noticed these resemblances.

"Hi Baby," Nina said as soon as Lela was in the room. "Help me with this, will ya? I'm a little behind in my chores."

"Sure will," Lela sang in a way that only she could do and proceeded to help her mother. She was always willing to do anything she could for Mama and in this case, happy to have a hand in the preparation of Papa's supper.

The time for Papa's arrival from work was so close that even the animals of the house knew it. They too loved and adored the man of the house. One would surely believe that they tuned in their keen sense of hearing. Some say that animals can sense things happening in the lives of their owners–even when they are away from them. Biscuit, Papa's ole hound dog kept looking up and around believing surely Papa would walk through the door just any minute. And, he was right! Just then, Papa's voice could be heard in the distance so regular, so welcomed and so loved. Yes, Papa was a ray of sunshine in the lives of everyone who knew him. He was so strong, so smart and certainly the best-looking man in the surrounding area. With the body of a lumberjack, his muscles were well defined and there was no fat to be found on him. At thirty-six years of age, he was a tower of a man who stood six feet and two inches. His hair was thick, dark brown and naturally wavy. Papa's face was handsomely rugged with expression lines etched into it by hard work and the elements of nature. Full masculine lips framed the great row of flashing white teeth that both Mama and Papa were so proud of. Sometimes to mischievously irritate Mama, Papa would grow a thick dark mustache. This just added to his charm. He thought Mama didn't like it, but actually she was a little jealous when he grew it. It seemingly attracted attention from the ladies. Yep, that's him alright. "This little light of mine, I'm a gonna' let it shine, let it shine, let it shine, let it shine." He sang. Through the door he came as always, singing the melody of a Christian song, and sporting a big smile on his face for his family. Papa placed nothing above the sacred vows of his marriage and his family. Oh, how Lela admired her father. She could hardly wait to have supper with her parents and listen to their many stories and be the center of his attention during and after the meal. Singing was a very big part of their lives. Papa always said, "If things are goin' good, sing a song, and if things are goin' rough, sing a song. Don't ever, and I mean ever be without a song." Lela didn't have the singing voice of her parents, but she sang in church, and any other place she might be. Papa was right. Singing was medicine for the soul.

Hugging and kissing his family, Lela's Papa greeted them with love and affection. They were a welcomed sight to him after a hard day on the job. He looked forward to eating, caring for his animals and doing a few chores around the house before relaxing in the evenings. Work time always seemed to come early, so he enjoyed every minute of leisure time with them.

"They're havin' a picnic at the church for the youth this Sunday afternoon," he said matter-of-factly. "All the girls from fifteen-years old and up are supposed to make a picnic lunch for the young man of their choice. I guess that since the gals are doin' the cookin', they have the right to choose which boy they want to eat it with. Now, Lela. Fry your best-fried chicken and do all the fixins just like your Mama taught ya. Whoever you choose is gonna be the luckiest boy there. Not only will he eat the best food, but he'll also be eatin' it with the prettiest girl around here. And don't you get too sweet too fast neither," he said jokingly as he winked at her in a teasing manner.

Sunday afternoon couldn't have come soon enough for Lela. She had busied herself all morning in anticipation of the picnic. Her hair had to be just perfect and what dress to wear was such a big decision to make. Not that she had that many to choose from.

God knows, she could almost count her outfits on one hand, but what clothing she did have, she cared well for them and whenever she was blessed with a new dress, she always bought styles that would last through several years. Since it was spring, she decided on a navy blue dress with a big white collar that was embellished with navy blue polka dots. Black was the only color dress shoes she owned, so she felt well dressed. Anyway, the dress fit her very well and somehow made her look a little older and more mature than her years. She had the dress, the picnic basket and an abundance of energy. Lela was more than ready. She wanted to wear her Mama's white picture hat with the navy blue band, so Mama told her that she could wear it to keep the sun from "kissing" her and making freckles on her skin.

With the exception of an old horse that Papa owned for many years, the family (like other families around) walked. They were no different from other families in the area. Lela felt lucky today because the church was close to their house, as was the small general store and post office. They always walked to and from these places and she and Mama would stop and have small talk with other folks on their way.

It had been raining a lot lately and the dogwood was in full bloom, as were most of the fruit trees. There was a sweet fragrance of spring in the air and this was just the perfect weather for a church picnic. Not too hot and not too cool. Beautiful!

A little tired from the walk, Lela and her parents arrived. Glancing in the direction of the church, she could see a rather good-sized crowd of people gathering. Some makeshift tables had been built and were on the church lawn. They had been covered with tablecloths for all the girls to place their baskets on. Lela looked at the line-up of baskets on the table and then she looked at hers. "Hmm . . . can I help it if my basket looks prettier than those?" she thought. A rush of pride ran through her at that moment. She certainly was proud of the training her Mama had given her on how to be a lady, look like a lady, behave like a lady and above all, be a Christian lady.

Several large old oak trees graced the property of the church. Some members wanted to cut them down, but the church put it to a vote and the congregation decided that they provided shade and the children were upset because bringing the trees down would destroy the homes of the birds and squirrels dwelling in them. Lela remembered well that heated discussion and how it ended. It was agreed that the trunks of the trees would be whitewashed to make them match the church and give them a cleaner look. She smiled. At this very moment, the trees were providing a great backdrop for a pool of young men. Lela had noticed them (without being conspicuous, of course). She didn't recognize some of them, but they seemed to be nice-looking boys. One of them in particular caught her eye, but she wasn't about to let any of them know that she was interested in the least. So, without a word, she turned toward the church door and saw her cousin Elizabeth, who was also a teen-ager. "Hi Elizabeth!" she shouted. After greeting each other and complimenting each other's dresses, the two young girls went squealing off to the church for a private chat.

Inside, she could hear the chatter of many different conversations being held by the many young girls who had come to the picnic. This was one of the most important days of the year, especially for the teens of courting age. They all groomed themselves, and had a day of "coming out." This was the one day every year that many romances were sparked and Lela hoped that she would be blessed with someone special this year.

Looking out the window of the church, Lela spotted the young man that had caught her eye before she came into the church. "Hey Elizabeth, who is that cute boy out there standing with Levy Cook?"

"Uh, somebody said his name's Frank Adams. He's been workin' for Walt Collins on a loggin' job. He's been stayin' with the Collins' too. That's about all I know about him.

Elizabeth went on about her way with that statement, as Lela continued to look out the window at Frank Adams. "Frank Adams. The name has a nice ring to it. Frank Adams," she thought and kept repeating his name in her mind.

Studying him from head to toe, she saw what she thought to be a perfect specimen of manhood. Strong, well-built, pretty teeth, sun-tanned skin, sharp clothes (and they were clean as could be), even his nails were trimmed and without dirt under them. His shoes were shined, he seemed to be mannerly and all the other boys seemed to be impressed by him. Whew! All of that in one package. If there were one flaw, it would be that he was not quite six feet tall. "What the heck," she thought, "No one is perfect!"

It was time for the picnic to begin, so everyone had to come inside the church to start the affair. The names of all participating young ladies were placed in a hat and the minister drew each name, one-at-a-time. As each girl's name was announced, she got to select the boy of her choice to share her basket of goodies. Lela held her breath as the first name was drawn. "If one of the other girls chooses Frank first . . . I'll just die!" she thought.

"Lela Pittsenbarger!" The preacher shouted. Lela could not believe that her name was the first one drawn! Not wanting to be over anxious, she took her time as she looked from one young man to the other and finally got the nerve to choose Frank Adams as her man-for-the-afternoon. She very politely placed her arm in his and led him out the door toward the picnic tables where she had previously left her basket loaded with a beautiful picnic lunch.

Frank, pretending to be shy looked at the basket. "If that food is as fine as the one who cooked it, it must be the very best. You're just about the prettiest little thing I've seen in a long time, Miss Lela." He picked up the basket and led her off to a grassy spot under one of the big trees. Of course it would be the tree farthest from the church. He spread out the tablecloth Lela had brought along and she began setting the food out on it. As they sat there eating and chatting, Lela noticed that there was something about him that was just so overwhelmingly attractive. She couldn't help herself. She knew that she was going to fall in love with Frank Adams, (if not already).

She hoped he couldn't hear her heart beating like she could feel it thumping in her chest. She didn't know it at the time, but Frank felt the same way. He too hoped that his excitement was undetectable. He was excited just to be in the presence of her, let alone be *selected* by her. He would just die if she knew. An over-eager man would not get the time of day from a young lady like Lela and he knew it. "Careful . . . don't blow this!" he thought as she fed him a piece of chicken. Was it the chicken, or her wrist that smelled better? He really couldn't tell. Both smelled delicious to him. Frank had become aroused and was finding his excitement difficult to conceal, but he managed. Just like most young men, he had become a master at avoiding this type of embarrassment. He changed his posture to conceal it from her.

For more than an hour, they ate and conversed. She was informed that he was from another county and was visiting her county to work. His job was for the next six months with Mr. Collins and then he would leave to another job. Each time their eyes met, both knew they would see each other again . . . and soon.

Chapter 2

More than a year had passed since the picnic.
After their first meeting, both Lela and Frank knew
that they would see more of each other. Their romance
blossomed quickly and intensely over several
months. Hardly a week went by that Frank and Lela
didn't see each other at least four or five times, and
most of those visits were serious dates. Knowledge
of the fact that Lela was the pride of her parents,
Frank charmed them also. Articulate, mannerly, hard
working and ever punctual, Frank proved to be a
prize for any young lady. When told that an evening
date was over, he always left in a mannerly fashion,
never asking for more time with Lela, nor did he
beg for extended visits. He knew just the right thing
to say and he knew just the right time to say it. He
knew exactly what to wear for every occasion. He
was quite a charmer. Frank and Lela soon became
the most popular "couple" in the area. The small
community where they lived soon accepted them as
an item. No longer were they referred to as Frank *or*
Lela, singularly, but Frank *and* Lela–a pair, a couple,
a union. Marriage was definitely in the stars for

Frank Adams and Lela Pittsenbarger. Local gossip now included the question, "when will they marry? Everyone knew they were almost inseparable. They went to church together, (when Frank wasn't gone home on "business," and sometimes he would be gone for several days). Frank ate dinner with Lela and her family regularly. They took Sunday strolls, went on picnics, went to local dances etc. No civic function was complete without their presence. Yes, "busy" is really not the word to describe the past several months of their lives. They were absolutely head-over-heals in love and that's all there was to it.

Lela's parents liked Frank all right, but since she *was* their only child, it was difficult for them to face the cold, hard facts that Lela was growing up and that they would (sooner or later) be forced to let her go. After all, it was the responsibility of parents to raise their children to become adults and set them free to live their own lives. Parents needed to teach their children the fear of God, how to love, be a family person, be a good, kind, loving parent, how to be a trusted friend and be as pure as one can be. If this be the case, then they had done their part very well. They were so proud of Lela and their intuition told them that if Frank had not already asked Lela to marry him, then he would do so at any time. Frank and Lela were healthy, young, in love and happy. What more could parents ask for their child?

It was Sunday afternoon and Frank had been gone "home" for two days. He was to have dinner with the Pittsenbargers this evening, so he was in a hurry. He could hardly wait to see Lela. Before he could go to their house, he must first stop by the small house he had rented. His stay in the area had been prolonged due to his falling in love with Lela, so renting a house and furnishing it became a necessity. Living with other people long-term was more than he could bear and since he was planning to marry Lela, they would need a place of their own. Providing a home for Lela would be of great importance when asking for her hand in marriage. The fact that Lela had already agreed to marry Frank was their secret. Now they had to share it with her parents. He planned to ask for her hand tonight.

Sprucing up didn't take him as long as he thought it would. In a matter of minutes, he was clean-shaven, his hair was groomed, his nails were clean and clipped, his clothes were clean and for the finishing touch . . . cologne. Umm, smells good. Frank had become a master at getting ready for dates. Looking into the mirror over the dressing table, he was proud of the reflection looking back at him. "Would *I* allow *my* daughter to be married to this man?" he asked the man in the mirror. With a final inspection, he felt ready for the task at hand. He winked at his reflection and strutted off toward the Pittsenbarger residence.

Whistling nervously and high-steppin'-it, he walked down the worn dirt road that would lead him to his soon-to-be bride. Frank was thrilled with the thought of becoming a member of the Pittsenbarger family. He had severed most of his own family ties a few years ago and as a result, there was very little communication between himself and his relatives. His parents were dead and he only had a sister,

Annie whom he rarely saw. Yes, bonding with the Pittsenbargers' was definitely a plus for him! He was ready.

Stopping briefly to obtain a small bouquet of roses from someone's yard, (there was no one at home and besides, they'd never miss them) he felt confident that his visit tonight would be a success.

"Well, here goes nothing," he thought as he stepped upon the front porch. Mr. Pittsenbarger's ole hound dog just barely lifted his head as Frank approached. No other response came from the family pooch. Frank's charm had even worked on him. So, with that in mind, he knocked on the door.

Delighted to see Frank, Lela opened the door right away. "Frank!" She squealed as she greeted him with the usual big hug and kiss. "You look soooo fine!" She whispered as she ushered him through the door. "Are you ready? She whispered. He answered with a flirtatious wink, which had now become his trademark. They were both so very happy!

The evening table was set with inexpensive china, but it was the best Nina had. After all, they were poor people. The napkins and tablecloth were homemade, but nice. Some pieces of the flat ware were of another pattern, but that really didn't matter. The important thing was that Frank had been invited to dinner quite often and this led him to believe that they just might accept his proposal.

"Somethin' sure smells good in here." Frank said as he entered the eating area. "It's been several days since I've smelled anything that good."

"Hungry are ya? Nina said with a smile as she

continued to complete her chore of putting supper on the table. She took time only to greet Frank with a small hug and pecked him on the cheek with a motherly kiss. Mr. Pittsenbarger shook Frank's hand and welcomed him to sit down at the table in the chair that by now had become his usual place.

After a wonderful dinner of meat loaf, mashed potatoes, green beans, homemade bread and apple pie for dessert, the conversation turned to asking for Lela's hand.

Frank opened the conversation with, "It's been and great evening and a fantastic dinner. I know we've all enjoyed it, but I have something to say to both of you, Mr. and Mrs. Pittsenbarger." As every eye in the room stared a Frank, he spoke with great confidence and determination. Getting right to the point, he said, "Lela and I have been seeing each other for several months now, and as everybody can plainly see, we *are* in love. We've been planning to get married since Christmas, but we wanted to give it a little longer before we jumped into something we might be sorry for. Now, we're *sure* we want to marry and so, I'm asking you kindly for your permission to marry Lela and for your blessings on our decision . . .. Please, don't shoot me!" He said as his eyes widened and he seemingly held his breath.

A moment of silence fell on the entire house. You could have heard a pin drop. Then, Nina spoke up and, with a big tear in her eye, a lump in her throat and a look of worry on her face she asked, "Where are you going to live? It frightens us that you might want to take Lela off to McDowell County or somewhere,

Frank. She's all we have. We just couldn't bear . . . "

"No, that's not . . . No, that's not our plans."
Frank interrupted as he reached over and patted
Nina on the shoulder. Looking over at Lela's father
he noticed how pale his face was and also saw the
worried, saddened look in his eyes. It was a look of
deep hurt and disappointment, something Frank did
not enjoy seeing. To hurt this wonderful couple was
the last of his intentions. "Don't worry. We're not
planning to move away. We just thought we'd move
into the little house I've rented for now, and maybe
later, if our family expands, we'll find a bigger one. I
like it here and I don't want to move away either, so
I just plan to keep working here like I've been doing.
To make a little extra money, I can go to McDowell
County now and then. We plan to make our home
right here. Please don't think anything else, and
please understand that we really do love each other.
I want Lela to be my wife and I want you to be my
in-laws. I promise I'll take good care of her and do
my best to make her a good husband."

"Lela," said Papa, as he stared at the middle of
the table and never letting his eyes meet hers, "let's
hear what you have to say."

A little low, but audible, Lela stammered, "Well,
Papa . . . I do love Frank . . . and I believe he loves
me . . . I *am* eighteen years old . . . it's not like I'd
be leaving you and Mama . . . I'll see ya every
day . . . Papa, look at it this way . . . you're not losing
a daughter . . . ya might be gaining a son."

Papa still had not taken his eyes off the center of
the table. "When is this weddin' gonna happen?" he

asked, still staring at the center of the table.

Frank took a deep breath and said, "Getting to the court house is usually a big problem, but we can get over there next week, buy the license and be married by a Justice of the Peace . . . all in the same day."

"Wa-wa-wa-wait!" Mama said. "Ain't this a little fast? You two just decided to marry, and now to get married next week! This is too fast! Now Lela, it's not that we don't want you to marry, but the least you could do is slow down just a little and let your Papa and me get our breath. Why don't you want to get married in the Church? I'm sure a lot of our friends and neighbors would like to witness your wedding– including your Papa and me. Lela Honey, please don't shut us out. I'm simply not able to make the trip to the courthouse. It would be way too exhausting. What do ya say?"

Lela and Frank looked at each other. She saw the pleading look in her parents' eyes and decided then and there that if she were to marry Frank Adams, it would have to be on terms that would be comfortable for her family. "Frank, it can be just a simple ceremony at the church. I've always wanted my wedding to be a sacred affair and not some cold event in the office of a J.P. I'll be willing to go to the court house next week with ya to get the license, but we can not be married until the first week-end of August. That'll give us three weeks, plenty of time to plan a small wedding at the church. Frank, you must understand. I want God to be a part of our wedding and our lives. Mama's right. We have to be married at the church. I don't need a fancy dress and one of your suits will do just fine. We don't need a big wedding party either–just us. The church can be decorated with wild flowers and flowers from our neighbor's yards. We can have cake and ice cream on the church lawn. That'll be more than enough to make me happy."

Frank seemed pleased that this was the only obstacle he would have to endure. "Sure! That'll be great! No problem! . . . Then . . . it's O.K.? . . . Do we have your blessings?" he nearly shouted.

Papa and Nina looked into each other's eyes for a moment and they both shook their heads in agreement to the marriage.

Lela rose from her chair and hugged and kissed her parents and then led Frank to the door. Staying longer wouldn't be a very good idea this evening. Mr. and Mrs. Pittsenbarger needed a little time and space to collect themselves. Their heads *were* spinning. They needed to get accustomed to the idea that Lela would soon be a married woman.

Walking out onto the porch, Frank started to say that he was sorry about unsettling her parents, but Lela placed her hand gently over his lips, kissed him goodnight and went back inside. Not much was spoken in the Pittsenbarger house the rest of the evening between Lela and her parents. Maybe the shock of this evening's news just surprised Papa and Mama to the point of putting them at "a loss for words." Lela figured "enough said," and stayed quiet. She cleaned the kitchen and went to the front porch swing to relax. She had no idea how tiring this evening would be. "Mrs. Frank Adams," she thought. "The name

Lela Adams had a nice ring to it. Hmmm." Soon, she was joined by Papa and Mama. It was late, but still no conversation, only harmonious humming and low singing of Christian songs was heard. After all, Papa had said so many times, "Never be without a song." Indeed, a song always seemed to work well in certain situations of life. Like laughter, singing doeth good . . . like a medicine.

After a few tunes, Lela excused herself and went inside to bed, leaving her Mama and Papa alone on the porch together. They sat there for a brief while in silence. "Lela is getting married." How differently that thought affected them. Seemed like just yesterday that she was six years old and playing angelically in the yard. Never did they realize how quickly time would fly by. How could this be? Lela had become a grown woman right before their very eyes.

Nina and Papa sat there in the cool, moonlit evening. Listening to the crickets' chirp and the frogs croak seemed to comfort them. They just sat there close to each other sharing the moment. They knew it was time to let go and allow Lela to try her wings. It hurt like hell, but time is a great healer. In time, their pain would subside. The cycle of recuperation would soon begin and things would be better for them. A soft, hazy light was shinning on them from the moon. They looked at each other with long-lasting love and compassion. Realizing the comfort each could give the other, they went inside to call it a night. Exhausted, they finally fell asleep. Rest, that's what they needed.

The neighborhood was soon buzzing with the

news of Frank and Lela's wedding plans. There was no need for formal invitations. Not only could Lela not afford them, but also everyone knew the wedding would be open-church and that everyone and anyone were welcome. Just as Lela had suggested, the ceremony was simple and inexpensive, the flowers were wild and beautiful, (not to mention free) and cake, ice cream and homemade lemonade was served on the church lawn as a reception. This was quite a treat as the weather was hot and the affair was held on Saturday afternoon. The church picnic tables were also made beautiful by spreading them with white tablecloths, which were on loan from several ladies of the church. Wild flowers adorned the tables and lots of color was provided from the various patterns of china borrowed from neighbors and friends. The most important part was that Nina, Papa and all the neighbors were allowed to share this very special day in Lela's life. She was a radiant bride and her wedding day was beautiful. Lela and Frank were very happy!

Chapter 3

It had been nine months since the wedding. Winter had passed and Easter was being celebrated. What a welcomed sight! The birds were singing, fresh foliage was on all the trees and the weather was warmer. The West Virginia hills were a glorious sight to behold. Mother Nature had put them into full-bloom. Wild dogwood trees sprinkled the mountains with a light airy display of fresh white color. Redbud trees were everywhere. Lela took a deep breath to inhale the delightful fragrance of wild honeysuckle, which wafted through the opened windows of her house. Their vines grew along the unpaved country roads, as well as along the back fence of Lela's home. It was early May and one could say, "spring had sprung."

The house in which Frank and Lela lived was small, but adequate. Many newly-weds had started a marriage having much less. With the help of Papa, Nina and a few good friends, they had sufficiently furnished the three-room house. Not the best of furnishings, but comfortable. One bedroom was all they needed at the time. It was not quite like living at home although. Even though she had taught Lela how to efficiently run a household, Nina had always been responsible for most of the chores, Cleaning house, cooking meals, washing and ironing clothes, feeding chickens, gathering eggs and tending the garden had become Lela's full responsibility. "Good grief!" Lela thought as she looked into the mirror. "I'm turning into Mama! I look like her, my life seems to be a duplicate of hers and I work just as hard as she does!" Lela suddenly had a much deeper appreciation of Nina. How her mother could muster up enough energy to do all the things required of her and do it year after year was beyond the stretch of Lela's imagination.

Lela was exhausted by the end of every day now. Her pregnancy had taken a lot out of her. She would deliver sometime during the first week in May. That was only four weeks away. The first few weeks of her pregnancy rendered Lela weak and sick. "Morning sickness" they called it. Vomiting every morning was no picnic! Thank God that part was now over. Lela was thrilled each time she felt the movement of new life stirring inside her. A bond had already taken place between herself and her unborn child. She considered this baby to be a gift from God and she was ready for it. Not much preparation had been done concerning the baby's clothes, yet Lela thought she had enough to get by. After all, she was *not* rich. She and Frank had worked very hard since their wedding last fall, and it had been rough making ends meet. Immediately after the wedding, they had harvested enough vegetables from their garden to make it through the cold season.

Frank continued working for a man who had a logging agreement. He had gone "home" every two or three weeks for a couple of days each trip. His return always brought some extra money. Lela was happy about that. She trusted Frank completely. All the hard work of marriage didn't matter. Just one look at him and every negative feeling vanished. Oh, how she loved this man! He was indeed perfect in her sight.

She heard him coming through the door. "Lela, I'm home!" He shouted. His voice could always light up her face. Greeting each other with the usual kiss, Frank touched Lela's belly. "How is he? He said as he smiled and winked at her in his cute flirtatious way.

"*She's* just fine," Lela teased

"I asked about *him!*" Frank teased back at her. "You're not having *twins* are you?"

"No, and *she's* just fine, thank you." They had no idea the gender of the baby.

As if seeing the baby's name up in lights, Frank waved his hand across the front of himself. "I think 'Frank Adams Jr.' has a nice ring to it."

"Uh hum. And I think 'Maysel' has a nicer ring to it."

"Maysel?'

"Maysel," She said.

"I've never heard that name before. Where'd it come from?"

"Mama had a friend years ago by that name. I think it's German. I've never net the lady, but I've heard her name mentioned a lot. I think it's pretty."

Watching his face to see his reaction, she said, "I like it, don't you?"

"Maysel . . . Maysel . . . Maysel? . . . Maysel," Frank said in different tones. "Yeah, I guess that's good, but we don't have to worry about that 'cause it's a boy!" he said with confidence. He really wanted a boy, but would be happy with a girl, so long as it was healthy.

It was now the fifth day of May and well into the week of Lela's expected delivery date. Nina and several friends from the church had alternated sitting with her. She had become unable to do her chores, so they chipped in to help. Lela appreciated their loyalty and devotion. The past few weeks would have been too difficult without their help. She had managed to prepare supper for Frank and had invited Nina to eat with them. Now that her time was very near, Nina had decided that someone would remain with Lela around-the-clock. Tonight, Nina herself would be that someone. No way was Lela to be without her mother until after the birth of her baby.

Frank arose early the next morning and went on his way to work. Nina prepared his lunch and assured him that everything would be alright. Looking back over his shoulder, Frank really did not want to leave, but knew that the security of his job depended on his attendance. Missing work was a big no-no. One could easily be replaced for the slightest offense. So, with that in mind, Frank went to work with his mind totally consumed with thoughts of Lela and their baby.

Right after lunch, Nina went in to check on Lela,

who had been resting all morning. Lela had spent a most uncomfortable and restless night. Everything seemed so crowded in her abdomen. She felt as though she would surely burst if something didn't give. Just as Nina entered the room, Lela groaned with the beginning of labor pains. "Oooh!" She said, seeming to be surprised by the power of the pain. "Good grief! Mama," she complained, "is it supposed to hurt like this?"

"Childbirth is no easy thing Lela and I hate to tell you this, but you've only just begun. Honey, you've only had one little pain. This could go on for hours before your baby gets here. Those pains will come a lot harder and closer together before you deliver."

At that moment Papa came through the door and could tell by the look on Nina's face what was about to take place. "Is she? . . . Is it?" he stammered. "I'll go see if I can round up Doc. Meadows and if I can't find him, I'll bring Mrs. Spence. She's delivered more babies around these parts than he has anyhow." Papa was practically tripping over his own feet on his way out the house. He was so excited, but also very scared. It was not uncommon for a woman to die in childbirth. "God! Please don't let that happen to Lela," he prayed under his breath as he hurried down the road on foot to fetch some help.

Papa went just as fast as his feet could possibly take him in the direction of Doc Meadows' place. It might take him fifteen minutes to get there if he hurried. Praying all along the way, he thought about the day of Lela's birth. Wow! Talk about flashbacks! He had long forgotten the many emotional feelings connected with that day. Nina had survived giving birth and she and Lela both were alive, safe, and healthy. That's a lot for any husband and father to be thankful for. And, he was! But here came the same feelings he had forgotten about, feelings that he had long ago placed very far in the back of his head. Feelings of fear flooded him. He had terrible thoughts that something could go wrong. Lela, the baby, or both could die! "No," He thought, "I can't even think that!" His mind was racing almost out of control. He was mumbling these thoughts almost out loud. "That just won't happen! It can't happen! I know it can't happen! I have to believe it won't happen! God's in charge! We must trust Him to get us safely through this trying time! Lord! Please help Lela! My daughter! My baby! She's my only child!" The words were moving through his head so fast that it made his head seem to spin. He was dizzy! Why couldn't his feet move as fast as his brain? So he did what he always did . . . he began to sing a song . . . a song of faith.

His feet had moved faster than he realized. Before he knew it, he was on the porch of Doc Meadows' place. Not an impressive place for a doctor. The paint was cracked and peeled. What was once white now was gray. What was once clean looking was now dirty and unkempt. Papa thought that a medical doctor should do better about taking care of his place.

Bang! Bang! Bang! Papa heard the sound of his fist on the door. It sounded like thunder on the door. He repeated banging once more before he heard Ole Doc Meadows stir inside the house.

As he came to the door, Papa could hear his sleepy, intoxicated, slurred-sounding voice say, "Hold on, keep your damn britches on. I'm comin'."

The door opened and Papa saw something he had hoped and prayed not to find. There stood Doc Meadows' scruffy, unshaven face looking at him, disoriented, drunk and undesirable. His clothes were filthy dirty and hung on his body as though he had slept in them for several nights. His hair was oily and uncombed. No, there had been absolutely no personal hygiene practiced here for much too long a time. Papa was disappointed at the sight of him. He really did like ole Doc, but there was no way that Doc was going to be allowed to see about Lela today. His darling daughter needed to be in the hands of a more responsible person. A person that was at least sober and one that could be obtained immediately!

"Wh...what's the matter Mr....Pitts...enbarger? He slowly slurred his words. Papa could tell by the way his breath reeked and by his appearance that he had been drunk for several days.

"Uh . . . Uh . . . Nothin', Doc. I'm real sorry I bothered ya." Papa said kindly as he backed off the porch and headed off in search of Mrs. Spence. Feet! Please move!

Almost running, almost walking, almost trotting, Papa hurried to fetch Mrs. Spence. "Oh, please let her be home . . . please." He was on the verge of tears, but held them back. He couldn't risk failure to carry out his part of this crisis.

He could see the Spence place from where he now was. There was someone in the yard hanging clothes on the line. He couldn't see her face but he hoped it was Mrs. Spence. Trying his best to move faster, he yelled, "Mrs. Spence! Mrs. Spence!"

"Why, Mr. Pittsenbarger, what in the world's the matter with you? You look like you've seen a ghost. In fact, you're *pale* as a ghost." He heard Mrs. Spence's voice say.

"It's Lela, Mrs. Spence. She's havin' her baby. I come for Doc Meadows, but you should see him. He's drunker than a skunk and even stinks like one. I just can't trust him to help Lela. He's of no use right now. I really need *you* to come with me this minute. Please, Mrs. Spence. Right now!" She could hear the urgency in his voice, so without hesitation, she put her clothesbasket on the porch and went with him.

When the two of them arrived at Lela's house, Nina was holding a cold wet cloth on Lela's head. The pains were coming a little closer together by now and harder. Mrs. Spence lifted the blanket to assess the situation.

"It looks like everything's goin good. I think you'll do just fine Lela. Try to relax as much as you can and as often as you can. And breathe . . . breathe, remember Lela, bear down a little with each pain and push. You can do it." Mrs. Spence said. Her voice was filled with confidence. They all trusted her judgment and breathed a sigh of relief.

Finding the situation uncomfortable, Papa decided to find escape outside. He walked toward the door saying, "This is really no place for a man. I'm goin' outside. If you need me for anything, yell for me. I won't be far away."

Several hours had passed and Frank was returning from work. He knew something was happening when he saw Papa sitting on the porch. Papa never spent much time at their house unless Frank was home. Approaching the house, he could hear Lela moaning and groaning with each pain. Frequently, Mama or Mrs. Spence would appear at the door to give a progress report. The two women never left Lela's side.

Shortly after Frank's arrival, he and Papa sat on the porch drinking coffee and indulging in idle chitchat. Mrs. Spence came to the door to ask them to readily prepare some boiling water and that she would need it soon. Leaping to their feet, the two grown men nearly lost their balance getting themselves around the side of the house to fill the order. "I'll need an *empty* bucket, too." Mrs. Spence called after them.

"Yes, Ma'am!" The two men yelled together, but kept on going. Actually, they wanted to be farther away than just around the corner of the house. Hearing the sounds of Lela's suffering coming from within was just about more than either of the two men could bear.

Quickly, they fetched the empty bucket and passed it through the door to Mama. "Papa will hand you the bucket of water through the back door. Put it on the stove to boil." Frank said. "How're things goin? He continued frantically.

"Well, it's goin better than I thought it would. Her water broke about an hour ago and Mrs. Spence doesn't think it will be much longer. I'll let you know." She closed the door and went back inside to assist Mrs. Spence. Momentarily, the two men joined each other on the porch to await the next delivery of news.

About another hour had passed, when they both heard the sound of a squalling baby come from inside the house. Up they jumped. Not being brave enough to open the door, they waited patiently for the door to open for them. Mama appeared in the open doorway with a big sigh of relief and announced, "It's a GIRL!" Expressing their happiness, the three of them hugged, kissed and hopped around like jumping jacks. So great was their excitement that they didn't care who saw them celebrating. Mama went back into the house saying, "Don't either of you run off now, 'cause I've got things for you to do." Papa sat down on the porch, leaned against a post and immediately began to sing a song. Something he always did. Papa always had a song to sing, especially if he was happy . . . And he was elated! Much to his surprise, Frank joined in with him and the two men shared a very precious moment in each of their lives. Frank had become a father and Papa had become a grandfather.

"We're changing the bed now," Mrs. Spence said as she stepped outside the door. Giving Frank a bucket, she continued. "Here, take this to the woods and bury it–bucket and all. Make sure it's buried at least two feet deep, and covered well. We don't want dogs diggin' it up and draggin' it all over the place."

"Yes, Ma'am," he said.

Taking the bucket, Frank looked inside. He almost vomited at the sight of afterbirth and bloodied rags.

"Yuck!" He thought, but said nothing. After all, it could have been himself (alone) having to deliver the baby. "Shut up and count your blessings," he thought as he headed toward the back of the house in search of a shovel. Papa joined him and the two disappeared into the woods to do the deed requested of them.

Returning in about thirty minutes, they were met at the door by Mrs. Spence. There were no sounds coming from within the house. She urged them to come see Lela and the baby, which they did without too much coaxing. Lela, lying there nursing her child, was a beautiful sight.

"It's a girl." Frank whispered as he kissed Lela ever-so-gently on the lips.

"I know." Said Lela weakly, "and I really don't think FRANK ADAMS JR. is gonna work. Do you?

"No," he laughed as he continued to admire the little bundle of joy lying in her mother's arms. "I couldn't be more proud even if she were a boy."

"Her name is Maysel, ya know," Lela said.

"I know," Frank replied, remembering the name games they had played and knowing also that he had lost.

Papa and Nina had been observing this scene and interrupted with their own comments of pride.

Mrs. Spence announced that she would now be leaving and recommended that Lela be allowed to rest for the remainder of the night. "I think she'll be alright now," she said as she walked toward the door.

Nina, Papa and Frank each thanked her, asking if there was a fee for her assistance. "Don't be silly, it was my pleasure. I'm glad to help in any way I can. Good-night," she replied and left the house.

Jumping up from where he was seated, Frank said, "Wait, Mrs. Spence. I'll walk you home."

Nina and Papa prepared to retire for the night. They all needed a good night's rest. Tomorrow would be the first day of living with a new baby. Their excitement was unexplainable. A baby! Wow!

For the next three days, Lela was totally exhausted and sore from giving birth. She was however, grateful for the love and dedication she had received from her family. She prayed God's blessing on the life of Mrs. Spence for the part she played in the delivery of her beautiful little girl. Lela was weak from loss of blood and from the hard work involved in childbirth. It wasn't called "labor" for no reason! This experience had landed Lela in bed for three days and it looked like she may be there a few more. Nonetheless, she could feel her strength (ever-so-slowly) returning a little each day. Soon, no one would find it necessary to stay with her. Mama had practically stayed by her side from the day of Maysel's arrival.

Looking down into Maysel's face, Lela thought, "Now, I realize the love that Mama has felt for me all my life. She often told me the day would come when I would understand the power of a mother's love. I guess that day is here." She then began to speak in baby talk. "Mommy woves you more than anything or anybody in dis world . . . yes, her does!" Maysel cooed and Lela planted a gentle kiss on her forehead. Sealed with a kiss, the statement was now confirmed.

Frank was ecstatic over Maysel! Every waking moment that he was not at work, or doing some chores around the house, he sat with her in his arms. His devotion as a father seemed to be un-paralleled. The love of this new baby had rendered Nina and Papa completely foolish also. They loved her as if she were their very own. They sang silly songs to her, talked silly talk to her, told her silly stories, (which she did not understand) and gave her their undivided attention. They were indeed thankful that both Maysel and Lela had survived the ordeal of birth. Their prayers had surely been answered. Now, they all just had to wait a few days for Lela to recover so that everyone could get on with their own lives.

Chapter 4

It was the spring of 1928. Maysel was nearly five years old and even more the center of attention than she was the day of her birth. She couldn't look more like Lela. It was as if Lela had been cloned. This child was full of life and possessed boundless energy. Climbing trees, jumping over small bushes, jumping off the porches, walking the tops of fences and now she could be caught sometimes walking the railroad track. Stepping on each railroad tie and counting them while stepping over them, she made a game of it. Games were a big part of keeping her entertained. Money was scarce, so any game that Maysel played must be one of no cost. The entire family revolved around her. Most of Lela's, Nina's, Papa's and Frank's time was spent keeping watch over her. It was a full-time job for everyone.

There were a few pictures of Lela as a small child, which Nina kept in her possession. They were Nina's pride and joy. They were never to be taken from the house . . . for any reason. Pictures were a very expensive item and Nina cherished the few she owned. Lela's image in these photos was often compared to Maysel, usually whenever Frank, Lela and Maysel were visiting Nina and Papa. The resemblance Maysel held with these images was uncanny. The same sandy blonde hair and the big bright blue eyes, these photos could have been taken of the same child and no one would be the wiser. Nina noticed that even Maysel's mannerisms were the same as Lela's. Sometimes, while watching Maysel play, a strange feeling would engulf Lela. Often, a sensation that only a mother, full of love for her child could experience would flood her inner being. Yes, Maysel was her life.

"DOWN IN THE VALLEY WHERE THE GREEN GRASS GROWS
THERE SAT MAYSEL AS SWEET AS A ROSE
SHE SANG, SHE SANG, SHE SANG SO SWEET
ALONG CAME PAPA AND KISSED HER ON THE CHEEK
HOW MANY KISSES DID SHE GET?
1, 2, 3, 4, 5, 6, 7. 8. 9.

Papa could be heard counting as he turned the rope for Maysel to jump rope. He could do this for hours, and often did so. Papa was the best when it came to playing with Maysel. He was so much fun and they enjoyed each other so much that other family members seemed a little jealous. Papa always had a song of some kind to sing. When things went bad . . . he sang. When things were good . . . he sang. During just regular days, he often kept Maysel entertained by dancing silly dances and singing silly little songs that meant nothing to anyone, except Maysel. And, when he did this, her laughter filled the neighborhood and could be heard all around. She loved him very much and since there was a shortage of other children around, she considered Papa to be her best pal. Of course she loved Nina, Frank and her mother, but she thought Papa was *really* something special. So special, (she decided) that no matter how long she lived, she could never forget him.

Frank was about to return from one of his frequent trips "home," so Lela and Maysel waited in anticipation. The extra money that came home with him always looked good. It helped to tie up loose ends, or was nice having it on hand for a necessity. He had been away for two days this time and they missed him. As soon as Maysel heard him coming, she ran outside to greet him.

"How's my girl? He asked. "I love you."

Always glad to see her father, she squealed with delight as he picked her up, threw her up over his head and gave her a big kiss. That routine was always expected, but she was also happy because he never failed to bring back candy for her. As Maysel hurried off to the edge of the porch to quickly inspect the contents of the bag he had just given her, Frank went inside the house and raced to Lela's side. He planted a big kiss on his wife's lips and she responded with her usual passion. It had been about seven years since she had met and married Frank and still he excited her just as intensely as ever. He could bring her to feelings that she didn't even know existed. Second to God and Maysel, (in that order) her love for Frank was the strongest feeling she possessed.

"Ummmmm, tired? She asked, breaking away from his kiss.

"Uh Huh," He grunted as he wrapped his arms around her, drawing their bodies closer together. They just embraced for a few moments and enjoyed the closeness they shared. Their relationship as husband and wife was spectacular.

"Better get ready, we're having dinner at Mama's and we only have about thirty minutes to get there." She told him. Lela went to the door. "Maysel!" She exclaimed. "We're going to Mama's. Come on baby. Put your candy away for later. We have to go now." Maysel did as she was told and off they went walking toward Papa and Mama's house. It was most convenient that they lived close to her parents. Lela was glad of that. They had no transportation except a horse. Frank and Papa were always using it and if the two families lived any farther apart, their visits would be few and far between.

"There's a photographer coming through tomorrow morning about ten o'clock, Frank. We have no pictures of Maysel and she's almost five years old. We should be ashamed of ourselves, but what can we do? We have to wait for them to come around and that's not very often. I guess I shouldn't feel too bad. It's not our fault. Anyway, she wants her hair cut before the picture tomorrow. I hope you don't mind. She doesn't like her hair long because of the tangles and if she's that set on it, I think we should cut it. What do you think?"

"It's all right with me Lela, whatever you and Maysel think. After all, it is *her* hair and if it bothers *her* that much, then cut it."

"Well, I asked her what she wanted for her birthday and . . . tell Daddy what you told me you wanted for your birthday, Maysel." Maysel would be five years old May 6.

"I want my hair cut and a picture of me. You know, like the pictures of you when you were a little girl." Looking at Frank as if to say, "See, that's what she wants. I told you it was her decision." Lela kept on walking. The decision had been made, agreed upon and would be carried out. Early tomorrow morning, she would have her friend Elizabeth to come over. Together, they would cut Maysel's hair. "I hope we don't ruin her looks. This picture will be her very first one. It would just be our luck to mess her up!" Lela thought. "Oh, well, it's only hair. If we don't like it, then it'll grow back."

Chapter 5

Monday mornings were always very trying for Lela. Her day always began the same. See Frank off to work, feed Maysel, clean the kitchen and then spend the rest of the day doing laundry. She had just finished washing a load of laundry and was outside on this particularly sunny day with her basket full of wet sheets, hanging them on the clothesline. This was one of the times when she had to take Papa's advice and sing. As she sang and tended her laundry, she noticed a woman standing on the outside of her gate.

Finally, the woman spoke. "Hello!" The woman yelled just loud enough for Lela to hear her. Lela was surprised when the woman spoke to her. "Please excuse me, I didn't mean to startle you." She said.

"Oh, hi there." Lela said, as she put down her work and walked closer to the gate. Lela didn't know this woman and she didn't want to seem rude. She continued walking toward the woman. Her eyes scanned this lady quickly up and down. Lela thought the woman was rather attractive, looked neat and tidy and might be just a few years older the Lela. She approached the gate and leaned on it.

"What can I help you with? Lela asked in her friendliest voice.

"I'm lookin' for somebody. Maybe you can help me." The woman replied.

"Sure, if I can, I know just about everybody around here. Who're ya lookin' for?"

"Lookin' for a man by the name of Frank Adams. I was told he lives here." The visitor said. "Does he? She asked.

"Yes." Lela said, with a puzzled look.

"And you might be? The woman asked.

"His wife, Lela Adams." Lela said, extending her hand. The two shook hands.

"Pleased to meet ya Ma am," Said the woman closing her eyes and sighing heavily.

Mimicking the woman's question, Lela said, "And you might be . . .?"

"I followed Frank from McDowell County last night. I waited for him to leave this morning so I could talk to you." The woman said, her voice seemed strained and Lela could tell by the shortness of the woman's breath that she was nervous.

"Why? Lela asked.

"We have something very important to discuss, Mrs. Adams."

"You still haven't told *me* who *you* are." Lela said, quickly tiring of this conversation. A woman has followed Frank home, waited for him to leave so she could talk to Lela? What could all of this mean?

"I don't mean to be rude, but," Lela said, "I really have a lot of work to do. My morning is getting away from me and I must get back to my chores. Now, if you have nothing further to say, I'm going to excuse myself. And, if you want to speak to Frank, he'll be home about six o'clock this evening." Lela said as she turned to leave.

"No, wait, I need to talk to you." The woman said kindly.

"Then please do so. Who are you, and what is it that you want to say? Lela said.

The woman was shaking by now and with a trembling voice spoke these words, "My name is Mrs. Frank Adams too."

"What did you say? Lela couldn't believe what she thought she had just heard.

"What in the world are you talking about? Lela demanded to know in a slow, low-sounding voice.

"It's true. I've been married to Frank now for more than eight years. How long have you been married to him? A tear came to her eye.

"Frank and I have been married for more than six years, but he never told me he was a divorcee." Lela was completely taken aback by this conversation. Even though her chores needed to be done, Lela realized this woman, was right! They certainly did have something important to discuss, so she opened the gate and invited the woman to come sit in the shade of the front porch.

"I'll be right back." Lela said as she heaved a sigh. "It's hot out here. We need something to drink. I'll go inside and get us some lemonade. Sit still." Lela went back inside the house, leaving the woman sitting there with a worried look on her face. Moments later, Lela returned with some drinking glasses and a pitcher of lemonade. Pouring them each a drink, Lela said, "Now, I'm not gonna hurt you, or shout at you and I don't want you to be frightened. I'm gonna listen and you're gonna quickly tell me all about this mess." Lela spoke kindly to the woman as if speaking to a small wounded child and tried to ignore her own pain and disappointment. Realizing that they both were victims and that this woman was not a villain, Lela sat down on the porch to unravel this complicated and painful mystery.

The woman began with, "Well, I married Frank eight years ago in McDowell County. Frank's a good man and we've had a good marriage. The only thing I didn't like about our relationship is the fact that Frank spends so much time working away from home. I know he has to work, and finding work around where we live is really scarce. Because of that, he works away from home."

"Do you have children? Lela had to know.

"No Ma'am," the woman answered, "we just never did have none."

"Go on." Lela said. Her heart had not pounded in her chest this hard since the first day she met Frank.

"Frank, for a long time came home every weekend." The woman continued. "Then, he started comin' home about every two weeks. He always brought extra money with him and I had no reason to think anything was wrong. Then," she paused to catch her breath, "Then, all of a sudden, when he came home, he didn't seem to be interested in me in *any* way. I couldn't do anything to please him. He found fault with everything I did for him. His clothes weren't ironed to please him. His shoes weren't polished to please him. Nothin' . . . and I mean nothing would please this man. One time, about a year ago, he struck me and knocked me to the floor. I still don't know why he did that. Our marriage has been rotten ever since."

"That don't sound like my Frank, but go ahead." Lela urged her.

"Things just got worse and worse. I couldn't stand it any more, so I decided to follow him. He don't know it, but he led me here." The woman had begun to cry by now. "I really don't know what else to say to you, Mrs. Adams, except that I'm truly sorry to be the one tellin' you this. It hurts me for both of us. I am sorry. Do you have any children?

"Yes, we have a little girl. Her name is Maysel. She's almost five years old."

"Maysel. What a pretty name."

"Thank you." Lela whispered. She was stunned.

"What do you plan to do? The woman asked Lela.

"Well," Lela said slowly with heaviness in her voice. "I most certainly can not go on like this. Mrs. Adams, I can't tell you what to do about your relationship with Frank, but I can assure you that mine with him are over. I love Frank very, very much, but I'll have no part of any man who makes a mockery of God and the sacred vows of marriage. This is just unthinkable! I can't believe this! Just like that," she snapped her fingers, "and it's over." She paused and spoke very slowly. "You'll have to excuse me now,

Mrs. Adams, but as far as I'm concerned, there has just been a death in my family. I feel like my husband just died." As if in a trance, Lela rose to her feet. She thought for sure that she was going to faint, but she didn't. This unexpected news made her head spin. So, without another word, she slowly walked back into the house and left Mrs. Adams to find her own way out the gate. Lela Pittsenbarger, married to a bigamist! That was the most scandalizing thing she could ever think of!

Still feeling as though she would faint, Lela closed the door behind her. Holding on to the furniture, she made her way to the table and sat down. This was almost more than she could withstand. There were many questions to answer and many decisions to be made. This situation would affect not only her, but also Maysel, her parents, her friends, and the church . . . THE CHURCH! How could this possibly have happened? Lela, (the saint) living in sin. Hadn't Lela done her best to live according to God's will? Hadn't she given her heart to the Lord at a very young age and been conscious of God's will for her life? How could Frank have been so deceitful and cruel? Especially to the ones he supposedly loved more than anything? Mama and Papa will be heart-broken and Maysel will be crushed. How was Lela ever going to find the strength to tell them that she and Frank are not really married? She had to make a decision and there was no way she could make it alone. God would have to help her make it. Lela refused to ever allow Frank or anyone else to shake her faith in Him. Devastated, confused and feeling totally alone, Lela placed her head down on the tabletop and sobbed. She sobbed so loudly that if the neighbors tried, they could have heard her. Her heart was truly broken. It was broken for her and for every one whose lives would be affected by this terrible news. At this point, she was glad for the fact that Maysel had gone to Nina's and Papa's after her picture-taking ordeal this morning. Lela really needed a few minutes to pull herself together and some alone time to re-group and collect her thoughts. She needed time to prepare for Frank's return from work this evening. She stood up and walked out onto the porch. Noticing the basket of sheets that she had started to hang on the line, she held onto one of the posts. Kicking the basket (almost off the porch) and collapsing into tears, she slid down the post and sank into a lonely pile of disappointment. Moments later, she stood up straight, threw her chest out and went on about her chores. How could she face this? One day she was happy as could be and the next day, in just a matter minutes, her life was crushed to shambles. Deep down, she knew what she had to do and she was willing to face it like a brave soldier. This was no time for her to falter and be a weakling. She had a child to rear. What mattered most to her was her loyalty to God and Maysel. She felt badly for the rest, but they could console themselves. Lela's life (as she knew it) was over. Now, she must spend the rest of the day in preparation. Confronting Frank face to face would be a tremendous challenge. She thought, "How could any of this be true . . . How could it be? In absolute disbelief and as if the weight of the world rested on her shoulders, she forced herself to function. Oh! How painful this was!

Chapter 6

Lela didn't prepare dinner for Frank that day. She gave Maysel dinner early in the evening and quickly cleaned the kitchen. She would *never* prepare another meal for Frank, nor would she do *anything* else for him. She had broken the news to Mama that afternoon, not long after her visitor had left. The two of them had a good cry. Lela could see the hurt on her Mama's face, but except that her family would always be there for her, Mama had no advice for Lela. This was a personal problem and one to be resolved solely by Lela herself. Mama learned long ago that when romance between a man and a woman was in trouble, one should keep one's mouth shut and retain one's distance. The two women agreed that Maysel should be taken to Mamma's house. Frank would be home soon and the conversation between Lela and Frank did not need to be witnessed by this innocent child.

Never suspecting a thing, Frank came home and entered the house as usual. "Where's Maysel? He casually asked, without an inkling of the depth of trouble he had entered into.

"She's at Mama's." Lela said coldly, starring at him even colder.

"Lela, are you sick or something? Supper's not ready." He said innocently.

"I'm fine . . . and supper *won't* be ready." Lela stated as she just sat down at the table with her arms folded.

"Great day in the morning! What's the matter with you? Frank exclaimed.

"I had a visitor today that just might be of some Interest to you Frank." Lela said getting up from her chair to stand by the window. She tried to get up the courage to look at him, but the disgust was overwhelming. How could she look at the man who had deceived her for such a long time? How could she look at the man she had loved so deeply and trusted beyond words? She didn't want to know his secret. It was too painful. She turned bravely around and stared Frank right in the face. He knew from her body language, facial expressions and the look in her eyes that this was a very serious moment.

"Who came?" He asked.

"Someone you've known for a longer time than you've known me." Lela said.

"Who! For God's sake Lela, tell me who you're talking about."

"Mrs. Frank Adams. Do you know her Frank? I shutter to think how many other *Mrs. Frank Adams'* there are. How may are there Frank? Huh? How many are there!" Lela voice was a little louder by now.

Frank, pale as a ghost just glared at Lela and very

slowly said, "Please, tell me what's going on here."

Lela took a deep breath, heaved a sigh and said, "Frank, don't try to play me for a bigger fool than you already have. It just won't work. I'm gonna tell you what's going on here and maybe we can make a decision about what to do about it. For Heaven's sake, Frank, can *you* be real for once in *my* life?

Lela told Frank about her visit from Mrs. Frank Adams that morning, about how the woman had followed him from McDowell County, about how long he and she had been married, about his striking the woman and about Frank *still* being married to her.

Lela told Frank what a terrible situation he had placed so many people in and that their "marriage" was in serious trouble. Frank looked as though he was in shock, but that didn't weaken Lela in the least. Her mind was already made up and there was no way his charm could work magic on her this time. In spite of how much she loved him, it was over.

"Why didn't you tell me this before we married Frank? Lela asked.

"I was afraid I'd lose you. I was afraid to get a divorce. That would have taken too much time and if you found that I was married, you wouldn't have anything more to do with me. Lela, you have got to believe me. I *do* love you." Frank said with desperation in his voice.

"So, you decided to have two wives, not be divorced from either and just expect *that* fact to never surface? Frank, what kind of fool are *you* anyway? Lela asked.

"I was already married when I met you Lela. I wish I weren't, but the truth is, I was. I know that I should have divorced her first, but I was so in love with you that it was worth taking the risk. Honey," He pleaded, "I wouldn't intentionally hurt you for anything in the world. Lela, we have a child together. What about Maysel? She's the only one either of us have. We have to think about her. We've got to think of some way to fix this. We can't just stand by and watch as our lives together just crumbles around us." He went on.

"Too late," Lela said.

"Whataya mean, too late? Frank asked. He felt sure they could patch this up some way. After all, they were so much in love and seemed to have the perfect life together. She couldn't be serious!

"Frank," Lela said painfully, "it's too late. I mean, my life crumbled to bits today. I'm sorry, but this is not just about *you*. How dare you stand there and make this *all about you*! Let me tell you what position *I'm* in and then we'll take a look at *you*!" She yelled. "I have every right to feel the way *I* do right now. *I'm* the one who loves God more than anything, *I'm* the one who would do nothing to make Him unhappy with me, *I'm* the one who has lived in sin for more than *six* years. I believe this has a little more to do with *me* than it does *you*! Further, *I'm* the one who trusted you beyond belief! *I'm* the one who had a baby by you and might I add, OUT OF WEDLOCK! *I'm* the one standing here without a husband and *I'm* the one who's been living with another woman's husband for more than six years. And, YOU'RE the one who is to blame!" She screamed.

"Lela, please," Frank begged, "allow me to *quietly* divorce her and let's find some way to salvage our marriage. Lela, we *do* have a good marriage. It's worth saving. Honey, please . . . let's not do something crazy by throwing away the best thing either of us may ever have. I'll do it. I'll divorce her. I swear it." He promised.

Crying, Lela looked at Frank and began. "Frank, do you have any idea how embarrassing this is to me, Maysel, Mama and Papa? Do you? She asked. "A divorced woman around these parts is just "damaged goods." It's bad enough to face *that*, let alone facing God, knowing that I have lived with you more than six years and I'm not even married to you. It's just too much for you to ask of me. I cannot just casually over-look this. I've made a decision, Frank. Now, listen good. You've made a mess of my spiritual life, my emotional life and my physical life. In fact, you've made a mess of all our lives in general. It won't be necessary for you to divorce your wife. I call her your wife because THAT'S WHAT SHE IS! I AM NOT, NEVER WAS AND WILL NEVER BE MARRIED TO YOU! This is the way it is. My mind is set and *you'll* never change it, no matter what you say or do." She said firmly.

Frank just stood there and looked at her in disbelief. He never answered her.

"First, understand that you and I are through. One of two things will take place here. Choice number one; you give me a quiet divorce and let me get on with my life with all the humiliation, or number two: I expose you to the authorities as the bigamist that you are and you go to jail. I mean it Frank. It's against the law to do what you did to me!" She paused. "Which is it gonna be Frank? Lela coldly asked him.

Frank was sitting by now with his head in his hands. Finally, he spoke, "I guess I'll have to give you a quiet divorce. What about Maysel? He wanted to know.

"Right now, she's at Mama's and Papa's. I'm going over there tonight. Start looking for a place to live, Frank. Maybe you should go back to McDowel County and try to save the marriage you have over there. "Or," she said sarcastically, "Since I don't know just how many wives you may have, maybe you could try to save one of them." She paused for a moment and then continued. "But this mess your callin' a marriage is over. Anyway, Maysel and I will stay at Mama and Papa's no longer than a week. I want you OUT! This is OUR home and the least you can do under the circumstances will be to provide a home for us. I think you *owe* us that much. I'll get a job of some kind, doing something. I promise I'll help raise Maysel. We'll come home next week. I'm trying to be fair here. I want custody of Maysel. You can see her anytime you want, you can take her for a day every now and then. I won't mind. After all, you are her father and I don't want to interfere with that relationship. *Ours* is over. Yours with her is not. Now, I plan to pick up the pieces of my life and get on with it. This has hurt me more than you'll ever comprehend. I doubt I'll ever heal from this Frank. Don't insult me by suggesting that we continue this *affair*. That's what it is you know. It's an affair. I can't begin to tell you how dirty I feel, I can't tell you how deceived I feel, I can't think of anything nasty enough to say to you and I can't begin to tell you how sorry I am for your wife. Knowing how *I* feel, I can't imagine how *she* must feel. She seems like a good, kind woman Frank. How could you? Here's the answer your question about divorcing her to save our relationship. NO! Frank. Trust is the main ingredient in the recipe for a good marriage and without it, no marriage will work. Since there is not a drop of trust left between us, I can *never* trust you again. There's just no use in trying. I'm going to pray that God forgives me and I'll even pray for you Frank, but make no mistake about it . . . we are *through*."

"Lela, we can fix this." He strived to get that across to her.

Lela put her hand over his lips and said, "I'm leaving now Frank. We've both said enough. I'm going to Mama's and don't try to talk to me anymore unless it's about Maysel. I've nothing more to say to you . . . *ever.*" She shut the door behind her, leaving Frank standing there in total dismay.

Chapter 7

*F*or the next few days, Frank stayed clear of the Pittsenbarger's home and out of their sight. Not only was he afraid that Mr. Pittsenbarger might have the desire to do him bodily harm, but he thought that giving Lela time to calm down would be a good thing. Besides, in spite of everything, Frank did love the Pittsenbargers. They had been very good to him and he was devastated by the fact that he was no longer a part of this beloved family. Frank wept bitterly over all the hurt and trouble caused by his action, but he felt justified by knowing that Lela would never have married him had she known his marital status. Why he hadn't divorced Edith (his other wife) before marrying Lela was a question even he could not answer. He did know, however, that the seven years he had known Lela was (and would always be) the best and happiest years of his life. He decided to do as Lela suggested. He would find another place to live, visit Maysel whenever he could and give Lela time to cool off, calm down, come to her senses and try to mend the damages done by his wrong-doings.

Lela, on the other hand was praying for strength to

get through this very trying time. Being a parent was one thing, but being a single parent in the year 1928 was quite another. Most people looked down on single mothers during those days, unless the mother was widowed. Lela was not widowed. She was to become a divorced woman, shamed, rejected and unaccepted. Being a divorcee made a woman undesirable, marked, no-good, worthless and cheap. Because of her decency, Lela had always been admired, adored and put on a pedestal. She had been considered to be the best daughter, the best Christian, the best mother, and the best wife. Now, that would all change! And it was all because of Frank's deception.

Mr. and Mrs. Pittsenbarger tried desperately to stay neutral in this matter. They did, however express their support for Lela and Maysel. Their hearts were also broken from this unexpected event. Papa played a lot of games with Maysel outside and allowed Nina to console Lela indoors. Neither parent voiced their opinion on the matter, but they did discuss it in private with each other. They had no idea what the answer was, but they did know that Lela had to sort all this out in her own mind and come to some conclusion about what to do about it. They knew that Lela (as well as they) loved Frank and found it almost impossible to believe what he was guilty of. Nina and Papa experienced hurt, rage, anger, humiliation, shock and a host of other emotions, but they also knew they had to deal with it themselves. Whining and allowing Lela to see their pain would only add to the load of undeserved problems that Lela had to carry. Nina and Papa felt that they should just be there for Lela and Maysel. They decided to support whatever decision Lela made and that's just what they did. Besides plenty of prayer and support, there was not much else they had to give to this situation.

Just as Lela had requested, Frank found another place to move into. There was a boarding house not far from their residence and so he rented a room. Being alone, all he really needed was a place to sleep, eat and bathe. Besides, he wanted to be close by just in case Lela changed her mind about them and he could visit Maysel as well. If Lela was never to change her mind, then he would simply leave, but he couldn't give up hope. He thought surely (with enough time) she would calm down, their relationship could be salvaged and their lives together would normalize.

It sure was lonely living at the boarding house. This was not nearly the life style that he was accustomed to. "I hope this don't last too long," he thought. "I don't know how much of this that I can take."

Several days had passed since he had moved and Frank was ready to visit Lela and Maysel. He had not seen his in-laws since the separation and actually, he did not want to face them. Up onto the porch of Lela's house he stepped. The door opened and out came Lela. Frank was glad to see her, but she didn't seem to feel the same towards him. She stretched out her hand in a gesture that said, "Stay away from me,"

"It's Sunday and you told me I could take Maysel with me today," he said kindly.

"Frank, I told you that I would never stand

between you and Maysel. I will never talk ugly about you to her and I never will tell her what a louse you really are." Lela said.

"What about us? Frank asked.

"Us? Us? Frank, there is no *us* . . . and there will never be *us*." Lela said firmly.

"My," he thought, "she seems too cold and distal. I hope this coolness doesn't last."

Little Maysel, still a bit confused over the atmosphere that existed when her parents were in each other's company took Frank's hand and went with him. The dysfunctional condition of her family seemed a little strange to Maysel. Things were not quite "right." Frank no longer lived at home, Lela was always sad and no one had any answers for her. "Too young to understand," they told her. It made her uncomfortable, but she said nothing about it to anyone, except Papa, her special pal. She didn't want to make waves, or worsen the situation by asking too many questions. After all, "children were to be seen and not heard." This, she soon discovered, was the rule she was expected to live by. And, so it was.

The separation of Frank and Lela had certainly taken a toll on everyone concerned, but Lela was determined that she would not reconcile with Frank. She had resolved herself to the fact that it was over between them and that she would just have to adjust and get on with her life. She was not at fault and she was indeed a victim of Frank.

Frank, on the other hand, was still optimistic about their reuniting. After all, didn't she love him and didn't he love her? What more could possibly be required to straighten this out? If given a little time, he determined that Lela would forgive him. Frank was very confident that everything would eventually work out for him. Plus, he still had his charm. What about his charm? When all else failed, his charm usually did it for him. Hey, a few winks, some heavy flirting and some serious courting would fix this right up. "It may take some time," he thought, "but I'm almost sure I can fix this."

Lying on the bed in his room at the boarding house was the extent of Frank's evening activities. Being patient was something he had learned during the past few weeks. A lot of his time had been spent on this bed thinking, hoping, even praying that Lela would give in. Nothing seemed to help. He worked, visited Maysel, took her for walks and visited friends. He tried desperately to gain Lela's attention. There was not much going on in the life of Frank Adams these days. He had lost his family. Not only did he lose Lela, but her parents as well. He really missed the binding ties of the life he knew before the "other" Mrs. Frank Adams made her visit. "Damn her!" He thought, "Why did she have to do that?

Lela kept to herself most of the time and her family gave her all the space she needed to recuperate and adjust to living the life of a single mother. Aware that the news had spread all over the community made her almost a recluse. Other than going to church, Lela had no social life. Her divorce would soon be final and she would have to begin living the life of a divorcee in a society that frowned on them. Divorce in 1929 was disgraceful, especially for a woman.

Lela had no idea how she would face this, but she knew that she must. She deeply resented Frank for bringing their marriage (and her faith in God) to an open shame, but she was helpless to change things. "God and I will make the best of this." She thought. "After all, He knows my heart and He knows that I am guilty of nothing. If there is any sin in my life, I've repented for it and He has forgiven me. I will not allow this to completely consume me, nor will I allow it to ruin the rest of my life." With those positive thoughts, she set her sights forward and continued to heal. Most of her days were spent keeping house, watching Maysel, visiting her parents and trying to increase her faith in God. Lela never once questioned God about this matter. She would like to know the reason, but even if she did know, she was helpless to change it. She really missed Frank and still loved him deeply, but she must get over him. This was an impossible situation, so she went on about her daily chores. Taking one day at a time, she intended to get through this . . . and she *would* get over him!

Chapter 8

Frank's main objective over the past few months had been to repair and possibly salvage his relationship with Lela, but she stood firm on her decision to terminate it. Not once did she weaken or give any signs of weakness concerning that matter. When approached about reconciliation, Lela's reaction was always the same . . . "No!" Frank realized now that she would never change her mind and so he made a decision about his own life. He would have to begin a new life without Lela and a new life without the Pittsenbarger family. It saddened him to think the he would never see them again, but he had no other choice. The truth was, he could not live in the same community with Lela and not share his life with her. He could no longer just visit Maysel for brief periods. He could no longer tolerate a daily dose of Lela's rejection. It was impossible. He could not, and would not do it. What to do? What to do? Lying on his bed in the boarding house in agony and without his family, he made a drastic decision. He had a plan . . . a plan that would work for him. No one else mattered anymore. He was all alone now and so he should think solely of himself. No one seemed to care a thing about his feelings. They all seemed pre-occupied with their own pain to even consider the fact that he was hurting just as badly . . . or maybe even worse than they were.

The weather was beautiful and there was a slight breeze blowing across his face as Frank sat on the porch of the boarding house. In deep thought, he had been sitting there almost all weekend, leaving the premises only briefly to visit with Maysel that afternoon. It was Sunday, he couldn't make a trip "home," and he had waited for the family to return from church that morning before going over.

Maysel noticed him walk through the gate and ran to him. She wanted very much to see her parents resolve this problem, (whatever it was) and get their family back like it used to be before her fifth birthday. It was now the middle of August and things had not been the same since May. Maysel was aware that something was very wrong, but could not begin to figure it out. Every time she was close enough to over-hear conversations about it, either at home, at church or in the store or post office, the conversations were terminated. It was as if there was some big secret that only she was excluded from. The tension was swelling with each visit from Frank. Maysel could sense that something big was about to happen, but had not a clue as to what it might be. Wait and not add to the problem might just be the best thing for her to do, so that's just what she did. She saw a frown of disgust come over her mother's face as Frank came into the yard. That look had become common on Lela's face ever since Frank moved out of the house.

"Lela," Frank said as he approached the porch where Lela was sitting enjoying the breeze of this very warm day. Lela was drinking lemonade and Frank kept his distance for fear that she would throw it on him. Walking over to Maysel and placing her in front of him (as if to shield himself) Frank continued, "The State Fair starts tomorrow in Fairlea. It goes on through next Sunday. Tomorrow is the only day that I can miss work to go and I would like to take Maysel. It'll be an all-day affair and if I take her, we'll be gone all day until late evening. It's so far away and I really don't believe it's possible to be back before eight-thirty or nine o'clock tomorrow night. If it's O.K. with you, then I'll pick her up early in the morning. Whataya think? He said matter-of-factly.

Lela never made eye contact with Frank. Instead, she stared out into the distance as if he wasn't even there. For a moment, Frank thought he was being totally ignored, and then she finally spoke.

"All day? Frank, she's just five years old. Don't you think that's a little much?"

"Not really," He said, "I've talked with her and explained to her all about it and she wants to go. I know it's a little much, but other folks do it, even those with more than one child."

Maysel was leaping and clapping her hands in agreement with Frank. Taking notice of this, Lela shook her head in agreement. "O.K." She said, looking at Maysel, "but try not to stay too long. That's a very long trip for a little girl." Looking a Frank she said, "I'll have her ready for you in the morning."

Frank kissed Maysel and winked at Lela (who paid no attention to his flirting) as he left and walked down the road toward the boarding house.

"I've got a lot of things to do," He thought. "Pack a lot of things, tie up some loose ends and get ready to ride." Frank smiled to himself and looked all around as he walked down the road, trying to take in the scenery as best he could. He inhaled deeply as he walked, trying to smell the sweet fragrance of the roses and other flowers that were in bloom along the way.

"Better get plenty of sleep tonight," he thought to himself, "tomorrow's gonna be a long hard day."

Bright and early the next morning, Frank was there to pick up Maysel. He had packed plenty of food and water to keep their hunger and thirst satisfied during the trip. Maysel was very excited about going to the fair. She wasn't quite sure what to expect about the fair, but she did know that people gathered from many miles around to enjoy it. She had heard there were lots of beautiful animals for you to look at and many other attractions. Ready to go, Maysel climbed upon the back of Frank's horse. Lela noticed two horses. Frank explained to her that since it was along trip, he didn't want to tire the one horse, so he was taking two. One horse could carry his weight and the other could carry Maysel. Then, they could alternate, giving the horses a break from Frank's weight. After all, the weather was hot. Lela accepted that explanation and Frank and Maysel rode off on their way to the fair. "This is gonna be a very exciting day," Maysel thought as they rode away, waving frantically to her mother until she was completely out of sight. Maysel was already having fun! She was riding a horse!

As Frank and Maysel rode up to the boarding house, Maysel wondered why they stopped there. Asked why, Frank told her that he needed to pick up some things, which he had forgotten. Being only five years old, Maysel didn't question her father. She had never been to the fair. She didn't really know what was needed on the trip. This day was to be directed by her father and she was content with that idea.

Frank returned with a few large sacks of his belongings and threw them over the back of the horse that Maysel was riding. There was much more room on hers than on the one he was riding. A look of sadness fell across his face as Frank took one more look around at the place where he had known so much happiness. He breathed deeply as they rode *south . . .* not *east*! "Oh," he thought, "how nice it would be to own an automobile." The year was 1929 and automobiles were few and far between in rural West Virginia. Frank had seen automobiles before and although he suspected it to be far beyond his dreams, he silently promised to have one for himself someday.

They had been on the road now for more than four hours. Becoming weary and tired, Maysel didn't want to sound like a whiny baby, but she most certainly began to wonder how far it was to the fair grounds. She had been told previously that it would be a long journey, but it couldn't take this long! The sun was hot, she was perspiring, the horses were sweating, and all of them were becoming exhausted. In spit of these factors, Frank continued to push the animals ahead, stopping only occasionally to rest a few minutes, have a bite to eat and consume some water. Frank calculated that they were about two days from their destination, so the more miles behind him the better. He had planned everything. He was aware that the traveling would be very tiring for Maysel. For that, he was sorry, but nothing could be done to make the trip more comfortable for her. They would sleep in the woods over night. He had brought bedding with him in the sacks and they had plenty of food and water. The traveling would come to an end tomorrow evening.

"Poppy," Maysel said to him, (the name she had begun calling him recently) "how far is it to the fair anyhow?

"Honey, there's been a change in plans. The fair was canceled and we can't go back home." He said sincerely.

"You mean we aren't goin back home . . . never? She asked in wonderment. "Why?"

"Maysel, you know that we take you to church, right?"

"Uh huh." She looked puzzled.

"And we taught you who Jesus is?

"Uh huh."

"Well, Jesus came and took your Mama to Heaven with Him and we can't go back." He told her seriously.

Maysel just looked at him for a few moments.

"Poppy, let's go back home to make sure Mama's gone." She suggested. By now there was a little panic in her voice, for she loved her mother very much. "What about Papa and Granny? She asked.

"They're gone too and we *can't* go back."

"Why!" She almost demanded to know.

"Because, if we go back then, Jesus will take us too." He lied. "Now, you don't want that. Do you?

Maysel didn't answer that question. Jesus had always been a symbol of love and kindness to her, but at age five, she wasn't sure that she was ready to go with Him just yet.

Religion was complicated to Maysel and sorting it all out was very difficult for her. It might've been because of her age. She had been taught a lot about the Christian faith, but *all* of it was not quite clear. One thing she kept to herself was that she believed Jesus to be a very nice person and she was convinced that Frank had Him confused with someone else.

Not to seem argumentative, she continued their conversation. "Where *are* we going to, Poppy? She wanted to know.

"Well, Mary, I'll tell you." Frank said, hoping Maysel wouldn't mind him calling her Mary. His intentions were to change her name to Mary.

"Mary? She exclaimed. "My name is *Maysel*. Poppy, are you O.K.? She asked. Maysel was beginning to wonder. Poppy seemed so strange to her. If he didn't know her name, then there must be something very wrong with him.

"I called you Mary because I think that name suits you better. Whataya say we call you Mary from

now on. Don't you think that's a prettier name than
Maysel? He explained.

"No! My name is *Maysel*. My Mama gave that
name to me. Nobody else has that name. It's different
and I like it. I am Maysel." She proclaimed, determined
that she would not accept any other name.

"Well, Mary," He said, trying again to push the
name Mary on her.

"Maysel!" She said.

"O.K. then . . . *Maysel.*" He would try again later.
He could not believe her stubbornness. "It's time to
stop for the night. It's almost dark and we need to
get settled in before nightfall. I bet you're worn out
aren't you?

"Yes, and I'm sleepy too." She said as Frank
helped her slide down from the back of the horse.

They had been on the road now for eleven hours.
Riding horseback was no longer fun for Maysel. Her
legs were tired and sore and her back hurt. A blister
had formed on the inside of one of her ankles. It had
begun to bleed and ooze, but she didn't complain. She
felt dirty, but all she wanted to do at that moment was
sleep. This day had been much too much for any adult,
let alone a little girl. They found a nice level wooded
area to act as home for the night and soon got settled
into their bedding which Frank prepared. Sleep very
swiftly overcame both of them. Frank planned to get
an early start come morning. Traveling in the cool
of the morning would allow them to put more miles
behind them than if they waited till later in the day
when the sun was much hotter. That afternoon they
could travel, but not as fast. With luck, they would

arrive in Wyoming County before dark tomorrow evening.

Chapter 9

*I*t had been a long, hot day and Lela found herself missing Maysel more and more. This was the first time in Maysel's life that Lela had been away from her for the entire day. Evening shade had cooled the temperature to a much more tolerable degree and Lela sat on the front porch in the dark enjoying the crickets, frogs and the sounds of the night. A barking dog could be heard in the distance and there was a rhythmic creaking sound of the porch swing as Lela swung back and forth. Looking out into the night, Lela was mesmerized by the light show displayed by the fireflies all over the yard. There was a lot to be said for solitude. Sometimes it offered a tranquility that nothing else could match. In spite of that fact, she was more than ready for Maysel's return.

Lela continued to sit on the porch and swing for more than thirty more minutes, taking in all the magnificent things the night had to offer. Becoming a little uneasy, she went inside to check the time. It was nine-thirty. "I'll just sit on the porch and wait for them," She thought, "They should be here any minute. If I'm on the porch, I can hear them coming

down the road." At that moment, she heard horse
hoofs coming down the street toward her home. She
watched as the horse drew closer to the house, but
she relaxed when she realized it was just one of her
neighbors going home. He spoke as he passed and
she spoke back to him. She swung for another hour.
It was ten-thirty! Lela began to feel slightly anxious.
Maysel should be in bed by this time of night and
Frank had failed to bring her home. She planned a
tongue-lashing for Frank upon his return and ran her
intended speech through her mind. This trip was way
too much for a small child anyway. That was her
opinion from the start. "Good grief! Where are they?
She thought. She was in a panic by now.

Eleven o'clock . . . eleven thirty . . . twelve
o'clock! Waves of fear and panic ran through Lela.
By this time, she was pacing back and forth on the
porch, going in and out the house checking the time.
Lela began to tremble. Where could they be? They
should have been back no later than nine-thirty. What
could possibly be wrong? Were they lost? Had one of
them gotten injured at the fair or something? Oh God!
Please, don't let anything have happened to Maysel
at the fair. Could it be that darkness caught them and
they could not see to get home? Could someone have
knocked them in the head to rob them? She paced
and paced and paced. She wondered, "What, what,
what could be wrong? The possibilities were too
numerous to even begin to mention.

Standing on the porch straining her ears, she
listened for the sound of horses. Straining her eyes
to desperately see through the darkness, (and seeing

nothing) she made a decision. "I can't stand it any longer. I'm going to Mama's."

Into the house she went and very quickly came back out with a wrap around her shoulders. She didn't need the wrap because she was cold, but she was now shaking with nervous chills. By the time she walked to Mama's, it must have been twelve forty-five a.m. She hated to awaken them, but she was worried sick. What could be the matter?

Lela hurried up to the door of her parent's home and loudly knocked on the door.

"It's me!" Lela shouted. "Mama, open the door!" She cried.

Mama answered the door wearing nightclothes and looking very sleepy, and invited Lela in. Seeing the frantic look on Lela's face, Nina knew something must be *very* wrong.

"Lela, it's almost one o'clock in the morning, child. What on earth's the matter? Nina asked.

"Mama!" Lela said, "It's Maysel. Frank was supposed to have her back here no later than nine o'clock and they're still not here!" Beginning to speak faster and sounding more frantic, Lela continued. I don't know what to think. I'm thinking everything. I'm worried sick and I'm shaking like a leaf. I'm just about out of my mind with worry." Wiping her mouth, she said, "Mama! Where are they? She began to cry as she ran her fingers through the hairline of her temples and across the sides of her forehead. Her hands were shaking, as was her voice.

"Now, Lela," Nina said drawing Lela into her arms and patting her gently on the back. "Just calm down and wait, now. You might be jumping to conclusions. I feel sure there's some explanation for this. I really don't believe Frank would put you through this on purpose."

Lela rested her head on hr mother's chest for a moment and slowly pulled back. "Mama, I've got a bad feeling about this." She said as she slumped to rest her head in her own lap for a moment. "A real *bad* feeling."

"What do you mean Lela? Her mother inquired.

"I've got a very strong feeling that Frank has taken my baby and has no intentions of bringing her back." She said. Staring as though she could see through the walls, or as if she was having some divine revelation, she slowly turned her head toward Nina and whispered, "That's it! . . . That's it, Mama."

By now, Papa had gotten up and was coming into the room. "What is it? He asked.

Lela sat there as though in a trance, but Nina spoke. "Frank was supposed to have Maysel back home before nine o'clock. They're not back yet and Lela thinks Frank has stolen her."

"Dear God!" Papa said, "You can't be serious. Surely he wouldn't do a thing like that. What in the world would he do with a five-year-old girl? I really don't think he'd do that. At least, I *hope* he wouldn't."

"What makes you believe he'd do that, Lela? Mama asked.

Lela answered, "I've had a strange feeling ever since Frank and I separated that he would do something. I didn't know what, but I never thought it would be to take Maysel away from me. Oh God, Mama, what am I gonna do if he has?

Papa took a deep breath, sat down and said, "Let's just wait and see what happens between now and morning. I just hope and pray that you're wrong, Lela."

"I do too." Mama said as she patted Lela on the head to console her. Mama and Papa were worried also, but didn't allow it to show. They sensed Lela was beside herself with fright, and they had no desire to add to that.

Morning finally came. None of them had slept much. Mama and Papa got dressed and decided that Papa would meet with neighbors and friends. They needed to collaborate about what direction to take in search of an answer for Frank and Lela's absence. Papa left the house and Mama put on some coffee.

It was a workday, but this was more important than any day at work. His granddaughter was missing and he just had to give it his undivided attention. He soon discovered that he would be alone on his search for Maysel and Frank. Since this was a workday, all other men would have to be on the job that day. Understanding that times were hard and money was hard to come by, Papa went back home to prepare himself for his journey.

Reaching home, Papa conversed with Mama and Lela briefly, gathered up a few things needed for his trip and set out on horseback in the direction of the fair grounds. He could make it there in about an hour and a half.

Chapter 10

Light from the morning sun woke Frank early the next day. Looking over in the direction where Maysel was sleeping, he couldn't help but feel sorry for her. Was he doing the right thing? Laurel Branch Hollow was one of the deepest and most remote areas of Wyoming County. How would Maysel adjust to living there? After living the beautiful family life style that she had become accustomed to, adjusting to life in the hollow would be difficult. Frank knew she would miss her grandparents and her mother, but Maysel was only five years old and he figured that forgetting them would occur sooner than one would think. At least he hoped that would be the case. Was he ready to assume full responsibility for a small child? So many questions flooded his mind, questions he didn't have time to answer right now. He had to be on his way with Maysel as soon as he could get their things together.

"Mary." He said loudly. Frank was trying very hard to change Maysel's name. There was no answer from Maysel.

"Mary!" He shouted even louder. "Get up, we've

got to get started."

Maysel, still not responding to the name Mary got up from her sleep and began to prepare to ride again today. Horseback riding had turned out to be more pain than pleasure. Her ankle no longer burned as it had last night. The blister had dried and was not bleeding or oozing this morning. She wondered why Frank was calling her Mary again today. Hadn't she explained to him yesterday that her name was Maysel, not Mary? Still, he continued calling her Mary and each time he did so, she corrected him by saying, "I'm not Mary. My name is Maysel!"

Very shortly, their horses were loaded and Frank and Maysel were working their way farther south. They continued their journey to Wyoming County. Frank pushed the horses a little harder than usual that morning, hoping that by doing so, he could cover a lot of territory before the sun came out really hot at mid-day. Riding such a long time made Maysel so sore that she wanted to cry. Paying no attention to her complaints, Frank kept the horses moving. Sometimes, he would put her in front of him on his horse, but that didn't help much. "Why are we doing this? She wondered, "And where was Frank taking her to?

Frank let the horses slow up a bit to rest and catch their breath. At that time, Maysel spoke up and said, "Poppy, where are we going?

"Well, I'll tell ya Maysel." He said, "We're going to a place called Laurel Branch Hollow. That's where I grew up when I was a boy. It's been a long time since I lived there. I'm sure the place ain't much to look at, but I guess the two of us will just have to clean it up a bit and make it livable. It's not as nice as where we used to live, but it's all we've got."

"What about Mama and Granny and Papa? She asked.

"I told you yesterday." He said. "Jesus came and took them all away and we have to go live somewhere else. If we go back, He'll take us too. Now listen, Mary."

"My name is Maysel!" She proclaimed insistently.

"Listen." He said. "Can you remember what I just told you about them? Maysel shook her head, yes. "Are you sure? He asked. Maysel shook her head again.

"Poppy, I want you to remember something too." She said. Poppy looked at her with interest. "My name is Maysel. I'm not Mary."

"O.K. Then, let's not talk about them again." He thought if her family was not discussed that she may forget them sooner.

Maysel took a long time to answer. She wasn't sure that she could never mention her mother again. Her hesitation to answer made Frank a little uneasy. Taking a little more time to answer and in a low voice, Maysel said, "I don't know."

Temporarily, Frank accepted that answer. He was aware that it would take a good bit of time for Maysel to adjust, but eventually, he had to believe that she would. She would simply have to adjust. They continued on their way, and not much more was said for several miles.

Stopping only to eat, drink and rest a few minutes, Frank and Maysel finally were approaching Laurel Branch Hollow. Maysel didn't exactly know what a hollow was, but look notice as they turned onto the narrow path-like road.

"Well." Frank said to her. "Here we are. In just a few minutes we'll be home."

"Home? Maysel said, "This ain't home, Poppy."

"It is from now on, baby. This is where you and I are gonna live. This road will take us to the house where I was born. We've got just about one more mile to ride. That's how long this road is. We live in the very last house at the head of this hollow. We'll have all the privacy we'll ever need. This is where we're gonna live. It won't be easy, I'm sure, but we'll make it, you and me. We're tough ya know." He made a fist and winked at her. "We made it this far, didn't we? He said, trying to humor and entertain her a little with his charm. For a girl her age, she had done exceptionally well on this trip. Frank was glad for that. Yes, Maysel must surely be tough. Looking at her future . . . she'd better be.

Chapter 11

Mama and Lela had worried and fretted all day long. Both of them had cried till they could cry no longer. It was now two o'clock in the afternoon. Papa had left about nine o'clock that morning in search of Frank and Maysel. Mama and Lela were getting anxious to hear what news he would have upon his return. They saw Papa's dog jump off the porch and they finally heard Papa coming through the gate. They both hastily ran out to meet him.

With a look of failure on his face, Papa said, "No one saw them at the fair yesterday. I spoke with several people that I knew. I asked a lot of others who worked on the fair grounds yesterday if they happened to see a man with a little girl fitting their description, nothing. Lela, I'm afraid you might be right. Do you have any suggestions?

"Papa," said Lela. "We might need to make a trip to McDowell County. Frank has that other wife there and maybe we could look her up. It's possible he may have taken Maysel with him over there." Tears were streaming again. "We've searched our brains all day long and that's the only conclusion either one of us could come up with." It seemed hopeless.

"None of us have slept since night before last." Papa said. "I've had a hard trip to the fair grounds. We're all exhausted. We shouldn't try to do anything else today. Maybe, if we just wait, he may bring her home. If not Lela, then I will go to McDowell County tomorrow and look for them. In the meantime," he said, as he went into the house, "let's rest, pray and wait to see what happens." Papa spoke his statement more as an order rather than as a request. Mama and Lela knew that when he spoke with such a tone of authority, argument was not an option.

Lela returned to her home devastated, exhausted, worried sick and alone. Not only was her marriage over, she was faced with the shame of being divorced; having no job, and now her child was missing. How she prayed that there would be a simple explanation for this crisis, but she feared the worst . . . Frank had stolen Maysel! Her feet seemed to weigh much more than they did yesterday. The stress on her was extremely heavy and she was finding it very difficult putting one foot in front of the other. Slowly, she moved her tired body through the door and sat down. Papa was right. There was no need to stay awake any longer. It appeared that that she and Papa would be going to McDowell County tomorrow. If that be the case, getting some rest would be the best thing for her.

Lela's emotions were flying very high at this point. Her hands were shaking and the thought of her deep-down, heart-felt suspicions made her dizzy. The sickest of feelings occupied her stomach, making her feel as if she would surly vomit. Using mind over matter to alleviate that feeling, she rose to her feet and began the routine of preparing herself for bed. Eventually, she finished that task and lay down. Her mind could not rest. Maysel's disappearance occupied every square inch of space inside her head and Lela cried herself to sleep.

Chapter 12

The second night had passed and no one slept well, not even the pooch at the Pittsenbargers'. Devastated, the three of them assembled at Papa and Mama's house early that morning. Lela was beside herself, Mama looked like there had been a death in the family and Papa was trying desperately to be the strong one and hold things together. The imaginations of this family could not conceive what life without Maysel would be like. Their lives had changed so drastically since her birth that remembering life without her was impossible. They discussed their plans for the search and each immediately began doing what was required of them to hasten the progress. If they were to be back before dark, they must leave immediately.

Mama began preparing food and drink for the travelers. Mr. Wilson, an elderly gentleman who did not work had agreed to take Papa and Lela in his wagon. Mrs. Adams had previously revealed to Lela about living near Welch, West Virginia. That area of McDowell County was small and with little effort and a lot of luck, they should find her residence.

After meeting with Mama and Papa, Lela rushed home. She would need to dress as comfortably as possible. This would be a long, strenuous ride. Requiring several hours to get there and several hours to return, Lela expected to be thoroughly exhausted from the trip. Snatching up some things that might be needed, she hurried back to Papa's house.

Loading the food and drink, blankets, pillow and several other items onto the wagon, the three rode away. Papa began a song and Mama stood in the middle of the road with a prayer in her heart, waving her hand as the wagon rode out of her sight.

Roads were not well kept in the year 1928. None of them were paved and most had deep ruts in them, which slowed the travelers down. Nonetheless, they struck out in search of Maysel. They prayed and sang from time to time as they traveled. Singing helped to pass the time and some of the lyrics to the songs gave them hope and encouragement. Remember, Papa always said, "Never be without a song. No matter what may come your way."

Hungry for any information that would lead them to Mrs. Frank Adams, Papa, Lela and Mr. Wilson began questioning everyone they met about directions to her house. Finally, just before they came to the city limits of Welch, Lela knocked on the door of a home. A very nice elderly lady with gray hair came to the door. The men observed as she and Lela conducted a brief conversation. Lela explained that they desperately needed to locate a woman by the name of Mrs. Frank Adams. She must have sensed the urgency in Lela's voice. Lela discovered that the two women attended church together on a regular basis. The lady willingly gave directions, which led the trio straight to Mrs. Adams' door.

As they drove the wagon toward their destination, they noticed how familiar everything looked to them. It was almost as if the countryside of Greenbrier County had been duplicated. It bore a remarkable resemblance to their community. As they approached the row of houses described by the gray-haired lady, Lela began to count them one by one. Mrs. Adams occupied the sixth house on the left.

"Four, Five, Six." There it was! Lela's heart raced and pounded as she strained her eyes, trying to detect any sign of Maysel. Her eyes scanned and searched the yard from corner to corner, every window and every square inch of the porch. Nothing . . . not a sign of her!

The wagon came to a halt in front of the house and the three frantic travelers lowered themselves to the ground. The ride had been tiring, but none of them seemed to care. Only one thought took priority, only one thing really mattered to them and that was finding Maysel.

They moved swiftly to the porch of the house. It was a small, three-room structure, which looked very much like the one Lela now occupied. Papa knocked loudly on the door. Lela noticed someone peeking out from behind a curtain in one of the windows.

"Mrs. Adams! Mrs. Adams!" she yelled. "Please answer the door! I know you're in there! Please Mrs. Adams! It's extremely important that we speak to you! Mrs. Adams! Please open the door!" Lela cried.

With a look of confusion on her face, Mrs. Adams slowly swung the door open. Halfway standing behind it, as if to be protecting herself, she looked at them. There stood the *other* Mrs. Frank Adams whom she had met a few months ago, with *two* men. Were they harmless? What would compel them to come all the way from Greenbrier County to see her? Was Frank dead? What could it be? Not sure of their reason or intentions, Mrs. Adams spoke.

"Mrs. Adams, what can I do for you? She asked meekly.

"Mrs. Adams. Frank and I separated and are now divorced. The day I spoke with you, I told you that my life with Frank was over and it is. Now, after several months of visiting Maysel anytime he wanted, taking her anywhere he chose, he came and got her Sunday morning. On the pretense of taking her to the fair, they left early Sunday morning. He told me to expect them back from the fair no later than nine o'clock that evening. Mrs. Adams," Lela franticly explained, "they never came back and I highly suspect that for some un-Godly reason, Frank has stolen my baby!" Almost out of breath from talking so fast, Lela continued. "Mrs. Adams, if you know anything about this, please, please, tell us. If he brought her here, please tell us. If she's here, please tell us! If you've seen him with her since Sunday, tell us! My God! Mrs. Adams, please help me find my little girl. She's only five years old! We don't know where she is! We're worried sick. Maysel is the center of our lives! Please help us!" She pleaded.

Mrs. Adams, shocked by the news, assured them that she knew nothing bout it. "Mrs. Adams," she said with great compassion and genuine concern in her voice, "I promise you that since the day I met you and told you about our circumstances that I have never laid eyes on Frank again. I just assumed the two of you had stayed together. Even though I am his *real* wife, I figured that Frank would forget about me . . . I mean, y'all havin a kid and all, it just stands to reason. I never had any intentions of telling anybody about you and Frank. That would only have hurt the little girl and I didn't want to expose Frank to the authorities. Then, he would be in jail. What good would that have done any of us? This is just a crazy situation that I can't figure out. I'm sorry about all this mess, but there's really nothing I can do about it except to pick up the pieces of my life, move on and try to make the best of it."

"Are you sure you don't know where she is? Lela asked one more time in desperation.

"No," said Mrs. Adams, "I told you I didn't and that's the truth. I wouldn't lie to you about something so terrible. I'm so sorry for you."

The two women embraced each other. They both were innocent victims in this predicament and each of them knew the other's pain, but Mrs. Adams also knew that Lela's pain was much greater than her own. Oh, how she wished she could have helped her find her child.

Turning to leave the porch, Lela became aware that in her haste to obtain information about Maysel, she failed to introduce Mrs. Adams to Papa and Mr.

Wilson. An introduction was made and the trio said their good-byes. They boarded the wagon and set off on the long journey back to Greenbrier County. Nothing had been accomplished in their quest to find Maysel.

Chapter 13

Maysel thought the long, narrow dirt road would never come to an end. On the way up the hollow, she took notice of the surroundings. There seemed to be lots of small houses along the sides of the road. Almost all of them had a small barn of some kind, which stood not far from each house. There was live stock in the fields, chickens seemed to run loose around all the homes and she observed children playing at most of the dwellings along the roadside of the hollow. As they rode by, Maysel and the children just stared at each other, but no greetings were exchanged. "Well," she thought, "at least there're people my size and my age here. Maybe this won't be all bad. But, I still miss Mama, Granny and Papa." She also noticed the thick vines of wild blackberries, raspberries and other berries growing along the roadside. These vines were so large that they almost hung out over the road. Someone could stand on the side of the road and pick them with little or no effort.

Finally, the road ended. To Maysel, it looked like the end of the world. The road just seemed to suddenly stop. Looking straight up the hillside in front of them, she saw it–the last place in the hollow. A small one-room dwelling glared back at her. It was unpainted, had no flowers, no shrubs, no steps leading up to it, (just a winding path) and it was isolated from all the other homes in the hollow. Up the narrow path toward the house they went, walking through the weeds. The small structure was dwarfed by the thick wooded area surrounding it. One had to really search for it to see it. Lots of weeds and brush were present. Stopping in front of the shack, Poppy said, "Well, Mary," determined to change her name, "here it is . . . home. This is where we are gonna live from now on."

"Poppy, my name is Maysel." She reminded Frank of her name . . . yet again. She may do lots of things in her life, but she would *never* answer to another name. Maysel was her name.

Maysel took a long look at the place, which was to become her home. Not in her wildest nightmares did she ever expect to be living in such a place. She was only five years old, but she knew this house was going to be cold in the wintertime and hot in the summertime. Only two small windows were present on the house and they were located on the front side. Frank dismounted from his horse and walked up onto the small porch. Maysel followed. He opened the door and they entered. The door creaked open allowing sunlight to fall across the dirty, bare floor of the one-room structure. Maysel noticed a pot-bellied stove sitting in the corner. It looked as though no fire had been built in it for years. Cobwebs and spider webs filled all the corners and every other small place they could grow. Just one bed, a table with two chairs and a few wooden boxes made up the furnishings. She also noticed a huge collection of long-necked bottles occupying one corner. There were so many. Why? There must be at least fifty or more. Everything was dusty and there was no water, however, there was a bucket and dipper sitting on one of the wooden boxes by the back door. At the windows, makeshift curtains had been crafted from flour sacks. A rod pocket at one end of the sack with a string pulled through it served as a curtain rod. Nails secured each end of the string to the wall. A stale, musty odor was prevalent as though the place had not been opened for several years. A network of cobwebs completely covered a broom, which stood behind the door. Nothing hung on the unpainted board walls except a few shelves, which were also draped in cobwebs. No apparent housekeeping had been practiced here for quite some time. It was very evident that the place had been closed for many years. Satisfied that everything was intact, Frank went over, picked up the broom and walked outside. He swatted the broom against the porch floor and against the posts. As he did so, a big cloud of dust flew everywhere. Maysel, being shorter than Frank and standing innocently close by, happened to be in the path of the dust and much of it engulfed her small body. She coughed and waved her arms and hands in protest, but Frank just laughed and went back inside, taking the broom with him. He was very careful not to stir up too much dust inside the shack, but in one corner of the room, he swept a place large enough to accommodate their belongings.

He quickly brought them inside and dropped them on the spot where he had just swept. Night would soon come and they would need light. Taking a quick look around the room, his eyes landed on an oil lamp sitting on one of the wall shelves. He walked over and removed the cobwebs from the lamp. As he did so, he found some matches behind it. How lucky! He set the lamp on the table, struck a match and lit the wick. He let it burn for just a moment before blowing it out. He only wanted to test it. No need to waste the oil.

Frank had to hurry to beat sundown. They were going to need some water and if they hurried, they could clean a little on the shanty before dark. Lots of work would be necessary to make the place halfway livable.

"Come on Mary," he said as he picked up the water bucket and headed for the back door. Maysel just stood there as if she had heard nothing. Frank turned and looked at her, but she still did not respond. "I spoke to you," he said firmly.

"No, you didn't either. You spoke to *Mary*, whoever she is." Maysel told him. Why was he trying so desperately to make her answer to the name Mary anyway? "My name is *Maysel*!"

"Well, come on anyhow, I want to show you where our water comes from." He said, as they stepped out the back door and down one step. A path, which was almost grown over, led them to their water source. A natural stream tricked down the hillside over some rocks and cascaded down into the spring. It was very picturesque and peaceful sounding. The foliage was fresh and nearly covered the spring. The running water made sounds like soothing music. If there was anything for Maysel to like about this place so far, it would be that.

Frank rinsed the bucket out several times making sure all the dust was out of it. When he was satisfied that it was clean, he filled it one last time and they headed back toward the cabin. At one point, the path branched off and went about twenty-five feet in another direction. Standing at the end of that path was a small outhouse. Maysel was used to outhouses, but somehow, she wasn't in a particular hurry to inspect this one. She stood there and stared in the direction of the plain, feeble-looking structure. Frank noticed her staring and decided to introduce her to it. Without a word, he led her down the path. He opened the door and let Maysel look inside. Thank God! The inside looked a lot better than the outside. Maysel concluded that she could live with it. Displaying a faint smile, she turned around and began walking back towards the house. Frank followed. There wasn't much more to show her about the place this evening. They were tired, they had a lot to do before bedtime, and they needed to go to the store in the morning. He would purchase household goods and stock more food.

Back inside, Frank busied himself by preparing sleeping arrangements for them. And it couldn't be sooner for Maysel. The past two days had been very hard on her. She was still exhausted from all that horseback riding.

Chapter 14

Early the next morning after their arrival in Laurel Branch Hollow, Frank began to clean. Sweeping the ceiling, the walls and the floors, he was determined to make the place more livable. Any item that was useless to them was discarded. Any cleaning magic that could be done with a bucket of water, a few rags and a broom was performed by him. He decided that the musty, stale odor could be remedied by allowing both doors and windows to remain open. After about two hours of cleaning and airing out, the shack looked and smelled much better. All the cobwebs and dirt were gone and Frank had made the bed with some of the bedding he had brought with him on the trip. He made a tablecloth from one of the sheets. Behind some of the boxes Frank had found some pots, pans and an assortment of cooking utensils. He created "chairs" by turning some of the wooden boxes up side down and placing them in an arrangement for living space. Other boxes made end tables and a coffee table. He sent Maysel outside to pick a few wild flowers, which he placed in some of the long-necked bottles that he had filled with water.

One "arrangement" was placed on the table and the other two were used to grace the end tables. "Presto." A little color was brought to the drab room. Now neat and tidied-up, a huge improvement had been made. In fact, it appeared to be a totally different place than when they had arrived.

"Well, Mary," he said, still trying to convince her to take on the name, "let's go out back." Frank walked out the door expecting Maysel to follow, but she just stood there. One moment later, he stuck his head through the door and asked, "Are you coming?

"You spoke to Mary. My name is Maysel." She said, setting the record straight about her name once again.

"Whatever! Come on." Frank said in disgust.

Maysel followed Frank down the path. When they reached the spring, Frank just kept on walking. Where was he going? In answer to that question, Maysel looked up ahead and saw another shabby place. This is the barn." Frank said. "It's not too big, but everybody needs an out building for their horses and a place to store their tools and stuff." He said as he walked nearer the structure.

Opening the door, letting in some light, Frank began looking around the place. He looked in all the boxes, on the shelves and all around. Finally, he said, "There's enough hay in here to last the horses a while. They won't need much until winter. They can graze all summer. We'll tie them up near the house for a little while so they can pick a lot of the weeds from around the house. At night, they can stay in here. We're gonna have to get us a pig or two when spring comes. We need some chickens right away. Gotta have eggs, and when they stop laying eggs, we can eat them." Frank went on and on about how they were going to make it. Maysel didn't pay a lot of attention to him. Being only five years old and not interested in survival plans, as her parent, he could make the decisions.

It was a beautiful day. The time was eleven o'clock and much had been accomplished that morning. Frank and Maysel locked their doors, mounted the horses and took off down the road that led them out of the hollow. Maysel didn't realize how sore the two-day ride from Greenbrier County had made her until she rode a short distance on the horse again today. Frank noticed how uncomfortable she was and tried to relieve her by placing a blanket under her legs. It helped some, but not much. In spite of her misery, they continued on down the road.

Soon, they approached one of the many dwellings in the hollow. This particular one was occupied by a black family. The Varney's were the only black family living there, and the first black family that Maysel had ever seen. The Varney home was considerably larger than Frank's place and contained several small rooms, which provided housing for their rather large family. There were six children, four boys and two girls ranging from age four to fifteen years of age. The older sons labored to help keep the family fed, the garden done, the animals cared for and the property manicured. Actually, their place was neater and better kept than most in the hollow. Mr. Varney always said if you keep the children busy, they will never be in trouble. He must have been right, because there was never a problem from any of his children.

Looking out over the fields of what seemed like endless rows of corn and other vegetables, Maysel could see the Varney boys doing their chores. The two Varney girls seemed to be busy too. One of them was sweeping the porch and the other was peeling potatoes for the evening meal. There was no introduction of the children to each other.

"Hey!" Mr. Varney yelled. "Is that you John? Leaping off the porch and walking rapidly as though he was seeing a long lost friend, he came over to the fence.

"*John?* Who's *John?* Maysel thought, but said nothing. Poppy seemed to have developed a problem with names.

Remaining on his horse, Frank brought the horse to a halt near the fence. "Yeah, it's me, in the flesh." He said with a laugh.

"Why, I ain't seen you 'round these parts in nigh on seven or eight years now. Not since your Mommy and Daddy passed away a few years back." He gave Frank a sneaky grin and turned his head to the side. Never taking his eyes off Frank's face, he said, "John Brunty, (his real name) you ole' scoundrel, where you been keepin' your sorry self for so long? And who's this purty little girl ya got witcha? He looked over at Maysel. Mr. Varney seemed to be such a humble and happy person, but he sure was black. His children were fortunate and had lighter complexions than he did. His wife was of a lighter color. Seeing a black person was something new to Maysel. There had been none living in the area where she once lived in Greenbrier County.

"This is my little girl." He paused. Finally accepting defeat in his attempts to change her name to Mary, he continued, "Her name is Maysel. Say 'hello' to the man Maysel." Frank said.

"Hi there. Mighty pleased to meetcha, Miss Maysel." Mr. Varney said, reaching for her hand.

Maysel extended her small, white hand and Mr. Varney took it in his big, rough black hand and shook it. Maysel was amazed at the gentleness of his touch, in spite of the roughness of his hands. "Hi." She said, retracting her hand back to the horse. Mr. Varney and Frank continued their conversation.

"Nobody's been up to your place since ya left John and we been keepin a eye on it fur ya. I wouldn't even let my young'uns play around up there. Reckon they knowed it was off-limits fur them." He said proudly. Frank knew he was telling the truth by the untouched condition of the place when he arrived there yesterday.

"I thank you Mr. Varney, I appreciate that so much." Frank said. "When I left here about eight years ago, I went to live over in McDowel County and then I went to live in Greenbrier County. I met and married Maysel's mommy. A few days ago, she died and I couldn't stay there without her, so me and Maysel have come back here to live. I figure the rent's free, we'll make it some way." He said sadly and so convincingly. He was such a good liar that Maysel almost believed him herself.

"Gee, John, I really am sorry to hear about that.

If they's anything we can do to hep y'all, just let us know and we'll sure do it." Mr. Varney said kindly.

"Well, now that you mentioned it, there is *one* thing you might *could* do. You know that great big hog pin you got over yonder, Mr. Varney? Frank said as he pointed toward the pin. ""It would help us out a lot if you would let us keep a couple of pigs in there with yours. I can't afford to build one and if you'd let me do that, we'll help you feed them and take care of them. Then, when I slaughter them next fall, I'll share the meat with you."

Rubbing his chin, he gave the proposal a quick thought, Mr. Varney then looked at Frank. "Is it a deal? Frank asked.

"I could say no to you, but it's hard to tell Maysel no. It's a deal. Besides, neighbors oughta look out after each other." The two men sealed their deal with a handshake and Frank and Maysel rode off down the hollow.

Nothing was said for quite a distance when Maysel asked, "Poppy, why did Mr. Varney call you John? That's *not* your name." This name game was about to get the best of her.

"I grew up right here in this hollow. John Brunty was my name when I was growing up. Then, after I grew up and moved away, I liked the name Frank Adams better, so I changed my name, just like I'd like to change your name to Mary." He said. "Everybody around here calls me John because that's what they all know me by."

"Frank, John, it don't matter to me what you want your name to be. Your name is *Poppy* to me and *my* name is *Maysel*." She said dramatically as if she thought he was deaf. Frank gave up and never made another attempt to change her name to Mary. What could he say? She knew he had chosen both of his names and in all fairness, she reserved the right to keep her *real* name if she so desired. He had failed, but that was O.K.

As they passed each family on the way out of the hollow, Frank (now John) and Maysel stopped to hold small conversations with each of them. Each family was given the same story by Frank (now John) of his whereabouts for the last eight years. He went on how he married Maysel's mommy and how she had died. Every recital brought the same reaction. All the families responded the same. They all expressed sincere sympathy and seemed genuinely saddened by the news of Lela's "death," but added that they were glad he had came back to live in the hollow. After hearing the story so many times that day, Maysel almost believed the crock of lies herself.

They paraded past many houses with lots of animals and endless fields of vegetation. Just then she saw it. A one-room schoolhouse sitting on a very large area of level ground. A large bell was attached to the top of a post, which extended from the ground near the door. In the center of the property, there was a place to play ball games. Some swings were erected. Maysel wasn't aware of it, but this building would be a very important part of her life during the next few years. This was the place where every child in the hollow (six years old and older) attended school. Deep excitement ran through Maysel.

"Poppy, can I go swing?" she asked.

"No, no," he replied, "We have to hurry. By the time we get our supplies and go back up the hollow, it'll probably be dark."

"Is that the school?"

"Yes."

"Am I going?"

"No. I'll teach you everything you need to know." He said and kept on riding. He had no intentions of sending Maysel to school.

When they got to the store, Frank (now John) took Maysel inside. He bought several large sacks of sugar, some yeast, eggs, bread, milk, oatmeal, flour, oil, soap and lots of other supplies. John's attention now fell on Maysel. The only clothing she had was the little dress, bloomers, socks and shoes, which she had worn to the "Fair." It was the same outfit she had worn to be photographed. The shoes would do for now, but the dress had to go. Asking the clerk to find some bib overalls for Maysel, he asked that they be a size larger so she would not out grow them too soon. He paid for these items, loaded them onto the horses and they headed for home.

After breakfast the next morning, John went to the shed and returned with a pick and spade. He and Maysel (now dressed in her bib overalls) walked about one hundred feet from the house to a rather level area in a wooded area. At this location, John began digging a large hole about three feet wide and approximately six feet long. He continued digging, digging, digging. The longer he dug the more like a grave the cavity was beginning to look. By the end of the day, the hole was completed. It was about seven feet deep and resembled a grave. Maysel didn't know what a grave was but she was curious about this mysterious hole in the ground. Dirt from the hole was carried away and dumped over the hill at different sites so it would not pile up.

"Now," John said. "That's done, now all we have to do is make a ladder to go in it."

"Ladder? Maysel thought, "Is he crazy?

John went again to the shed and returned with some nails and a hammer. He also brought a small handsaw with him. He gathered enough tree branches from the surrounding area, made a ladder and dropped it into the hole. The stability of the ladder was tested by John's weight. He lowered himself down into the hole. Yep, it passed. He then gathered enough saplings from the nearby, wooded area, wove them together and fashioned a "lid." It covered the entire hole. Next, he gathered more saplings, twigs and other objects from the woods and attached these items to the "lid" also. When the "lid" was in place, the hole became undetectable. The property appeared un-disturbed, just as John had hoped it would.

Tomorrow, Maysel would begin to understand the purpose of the hole, but for now she remained very confused.

Chapter 15

John Brunty (alias Frank Adams) and Maysel had toiled very hard and long hours since moving into the hollow, and they had finally gotten the old shack in living condition. Not one neighbor had asked the first question about their previous life in Greenbrier County. They just accepted the story John had told them and there was no reason to doubt him. He had been gone for several years and when he returned, he had a little girl with him. The pieces fit, so why question it?

They kept mostly to themselves and avoided socializing. John wasn't interested in having a lot of company at the shack. Too many people would surely spoil his plans and he couldn't afford that. In spite of the hard times, he had to survive and the source of his and Maysel's survival must be kept a secret from the public.

Three weeks had now gone by. The shack was livable. John had purchased two pigs and was keeping them in the pen with Mr. Varney's pigs. He had managed to round up several chickens as well. He tied a long string to one leg of each chicken, the other end he tied to a stake, which he had driven into the ground. This allowed the chickens to walk about "freely." By feeding them corn every day for about two weeks, the chickens could then be set free of the string and they would not run away. Chickens will stay where they feel safe and near their food source.

Maysel still had a yearning to see her mother and at times was very homesick. She missed Papa, who had played many hours with her, and Granny, who had spoiled her daily. Although she was an only child, she had several friends at church that she missed greatly. John recognized her demise and tried his best to keep her busy.

It was too hate in the season for them to plant a garden, so John felt it necessary to concentrate on the "business." He had a plan that would benefit him tremendously. Leaving Maysel without supervision to work away from home was not an option. Right now, he had to find a way to make a living at home. He may be able to leave her alone for short periods of time next spring, after she had been here for a while and everything was familiar to her. For now, he was about to teach Maysel the "business."

Motioning for Maysel to follow him outside, John led her into the woods. There were several trails leading off into different directions. John took one of them and Maysel followed. The trail led up to a tall cliff. It appeared to be a solid rock wall about thirty or forty feet tall and about thirty feet wide. A huge crack down the center of the rock cliff made it look like two very large stones. Some sapling trees grew rather close to the cavernous opening making it hard to detect. John parted the saplings to reveal a wide opening made by the large separation in the cliff. Motioning her to follow him inside, Maysel gawked in amazement.

"Wow! What a cool place to play. This is a real hiding place." She thought.

No one would ever guess there was a natural cave here. As they entered the cave, John lit an oil lamp, which was sitting in the floor of the cave. As he did so, Maysel saw something she didn't recognize. Something that looked like a huge metal pot with a lid tightly secured on it was sitting in the middle of the floor inside the cave. There was a curly tube winding and curling from the top of it. The curly tube extended in a downward direction and wove through some natural running water. The stream came from outside the cave and then exited the cave and continued on down the hillside. This was the stream that fed the spring from which they got their water supply.

At the end of the curly tube (called a "worm") was a large bucket. The end of the "worm" hung over the bucket. Ashes from burned logs lay underneath the large closed-lid pot. A circle of stones, which looked like they could keep a fire under control, created a safety zone. At the top of the cave was a natural opening, which pulled the smoke out of the cave when a fire was built. Several large barrels stood along the back wall. Maysel wandered over to where they were, lifted up one of the lids and just about lost her balance from the smell. All of this was housed and protected by the cave.

"Peeeew! Poppy, what is that?" Maysel asked as she reached for her nose.

"This is a moonshine still, baby. Did you ever hear of moonshine? He asked.

"No. I don't know what that is." Maysel said innocently.

"Well, I'll tell ya about it. Moonshine is a drink that only men who live in the mountains drink. We have to make it, 'cause you can't buy it in the stores. I've got a lot of friends to make it for and if I don't make it for them, they get real mad at me." He said. John had to introduce Maysel to the moonshine business very slowly and he didn't want Maysel to know that these activities were wrong. "Maysel, don't ever tell anybody about this place, cause if you do they'll come and take me away and you'll never see me again either. Do you understand what I'm tellin' ya? You can't never tell nobody about this cave." He stressed to her.

She had already lost her mother and grandparents. Maysel didn't want to lose Poppy too. She shook her head and said, "O.K."

"Are you sure you understand? There are certain things that we can not talk about to anybody. We can not tell a living soul about this place and if any body should ask questions about . . . well . . . moonshine and stuff, just don't tell them nothin', O.K? He wanted to be sure she understood and that he could trust her not to tell.

"O.K. Poppy, I won't tell," she said

"Do you promise and cross your heart? He asked.

"I promise and cross my heart." She vowed, crossing her innocent heart with her finger.

They left the cave and headed back down the path. John led Maysel to the "hole" that he had previously dug. The one that he had camouflaged with a "lid" fashioned from saplings and brush. He had done such a good job of concealing the "hole" that he had a little trouble finding it himself. Stopping just a couple of feet from the "lid," he told Maysel to practice opening it. It was very heavy for her, but Maysel finally managed to lift the "lid."

"Great!" Poppy said, "Now I want you to practice going up and down the ladder. Doing as Poppy requested, Maysel climbed up and down the ladder several times. Each time she did, he praised her greatly. Finally, he told her to stand by him and she obeyed. . "Now, Maysel, from the front of the house, we can see almost half-way down the hollow. When I'm not home and you're here by yourself, if you see anybody coming up here that you don't know, I want you to go and get in this hole. Now, let's practice that, O.K.? Let's pretend that you don't know me and it looks like I'm coming up here. What would you do? Now, remember, I'm a stranger." John didn't want State Revenuers to be talking to Maysel.

They backed away from the "hole," almost half way to the cabin. John decided that was far enough. "And, if you ever have to get in the hole, I want you to stay there and don't come out for nobody but me. O.K?" he said. Now, you see a stranger comin toward the house and you are here alone. Show me what you would do." He said.

Without hesitation, Maysel went straight to the hole and with great effort lifted the lid. Down the ladder she went and let the lid down. John went over to where he knew she could hear him and said, "Now this is important. No matter what anyone says, even me, don't come out unless you hear my voice say, 'Maysel, come out'. Got that?"

"O.K." She answered. It was dark and a little cool in the hole. Maysel didn't mind the coolness, but she didn't care for the darkness. Anyway, she was having fun. What great places to play. This *was* fun!" She thought.

John rehearsed several phrases trying to get Maysel to come out. She remained silent and out of sight. Finally, he said, "Maysel, come out!" The lid to the hole raised and Maysel emerged. John praised her and praised her. What a good girl she was! How well she had followed his instructions.

Of course, Maysel thought this was all a game. This was big-time *"hide-and-go-seek."* She thought Poppy was playing games with her and she was thoroughly enjoying every minute of it. Little did she know that this game would soon evolve into hard work and that its duration would last for more than eight years! At that moment, she was just playing and pleasing Poppy. He was all she had now.

At night, Poppy slept in the bed while Maysel slept on a pallet on the floor. Maysel didn't like the floor. There were cracks between the boards. Maybe she could have a bed someday.

Maysel never forgot to say her prayers at night, something her mother had taught her to do. Each time she prayed, she always mentioned her mother and her grandparents in those prayers. John never commented one way or the other concerning Maysel praying, although he suspected that she never really believed them to be dead. Alone and in the dark, Maysel cried herself to sleep more nights than not, but John never knew it. She missed her family.

Chapter 16

*T*he leaves of late October had turned into a glorious display of color, and the trees appeared to have been decorated with shreds of gold. The mountains surrounding Laurel Branch Hollow were magnificent, in color as well as size. The weather was no longer hot as it had been back in August when Maysel first came to Laurel Branch. Temperatures had changed from sweltering hot to pleasantly cool. Maysel loved to play in the fallen leaves. She was fascinated by the way the wind would pick them up, swirl them around and set them down in various different piles. Having little to play with, things of nature became her toys. Outdoors was Maysel's favorite place to be, but soon that would all change. Winter was about to set in.

John had done a very good job at keeping Maysel busy and guarding her from becoming too friendly with neighbors. She had learned plenty to keep her occupied. He had taught her how to gather eggs, kill and clean a chicken, pick corn (and shuck it), sweep, carry water from the spring, help him feed the horses, and many other common tasks performed by mountain people. Maysel was a little young to be doing some of these duties, but John needed her assistance and was very strict. If they were to survive, then their survival depended on working together.

The most beneficial thing so far that Maysel had learned was how to "shine." Someone who makes, bottles and sells moonshine, (a home-made whiskey) "shines."

He had instructed her how to "run off" the "recipe" one-step-at-a-time. First, gather the corn and put it into the large smelly barrels she had found in the cave and mix in the right amount of sugar, yeast and water. Then, place a cover over the barrels and let this mixture set, undisturbed for several days, checking it from time to time. When the mixture had fermented, and smelled rotten, it had a very distinct smell and was called "mash." The "mash" was then transferred into the "still" (the pot with lid and curly copper tube. A fire was built under the pot and the fermented mixture was cooked.

As the mixture cooked, the steam was trapped under the lid of the huge pot and allowed to travel up through the curly copper tube (worm). The "worm" snaked its way through the natural spring water, which ran through the cave. By the time the steam made its way to the end of the "worm," it had condensed back into a liquid, MOONSHINE. A large bucket collected the product as it slowly ran from the end of the "worm." When there was enough "shine" in the bucket, Maysel was taught to dip it out of the bucket and fill each long-necked bottle and very carefully push a cork down into the top of the bottle. After filling as many bottles as the "run" would produce, she carried them to the "hole" and stored them there. When Poppy had a sale for the "shine" all he had to do was go the "hole" and take whatever he needed. By Christmas, Maysel would have manufactured enough "shine" to last until spring and most of it had been produced without John's presence. Now that she had adjusted to living here, John thought nothing of leaving her alone for several hours during the day. He knew that she would be productive and keep his stock up, while he was busy finding a sale for it. Thus, his living was being made by a six-year-old girl whose name was Maysel . . . his own little girl!

The "business" was going great and John was saving lots of money. A portion of the money went for buying more sugar, yeast, and other commodities, but most of it was pocketed. His plan was coming to life. Making this decision was turning out to be not so bad. He didn't have to work. Maysel worked and he had a bittersweet taste in his mouth to think that Lela, somehow, would hurt from this. "That's what she gets," he thought, "for rejecting me. No Frank . . . no marriage . . . no Maysel! If that's what she wanted, then she sure got it!"

Snow was now on the ground about four to six inches deep and had been for several days. As far as she could see, the dark limbs of the bare trees were enhanced by the glittery snow, creating a winter wonderland. The view from the shack resembled a huge Christmas card. If ever they had wished for a white Christmas, this was it and *cold* was not the word to describe it. The good thing was that John and

Maysel had cut and stacked plenty of wood before winter. The old pot-bellied stove in the corner of the room was their only source of heat, and further, it was all they had to cook on. A pot of beans and a small coffee pot continually rested on top of the stove. A good fire would heat the room very well just before bedtime, but by morning, the fire would be nearly out, rendering the shack cold again. Maysel shivered, but John would always try to rekindle the heat before allowing Maysel to get up from her bed on the floor.

Christmas Day may as well have been just another day for Maysel. Although she had worked like a beast of burden for more than four months, she received very little for Christmas. A piece of fruit, some hard candy, gum drops and wouldn't you know it . . . another pair of bib overalls, a T-shirt and a new pair of leather high top work shoes. A shirt and bibs, of course, was her wardrobe for the next eight years. She only got another "outfit" of clothes as she grew and the "outfit" was always the same.

The little dress that she wore when she was taken from her mother was the only dress she owned. Maysel kept it hidden underneath her pallet on the floor and from time to time, (when Poppy was gone) she took it out and put it on. Prancing around the room and singing songs that she had learned from Papa had become her favorite past time. By now, the little dress was wrinkled, but it mattered not to her in the least. She loved it. It was her most prized possession. This was the dress worn by her in her birthday picture . . . the one she never got to see. Poppy took her away before the picture was delivered.

Although she still thought about her family on a daily basis, the times when she put on the dress were when she reminisced about home and missed her family the most. Watching closely for John's return, she would quickly change back into her bibs and T-shirt. He never knew about these times, because she reserved these times for herself. These were the times when she could mentally escape and be back with her mother and grandparents. How badly she missed them and she would never forget them in spite of her young age.

Chapter 17

Life at the Pittsenbargers' had become a total and complete nightmare. Mamma and Papa Pittsenbarger not only had to grieve the loss of their beloved granddaughter, Maysel, who had been missing now for more than four months, but the Holidays had been heartbreaking. Thanksgiving Day had come and gone and so had Christmas . . . without her! These had been some of the saddest days in their lives. When the only child of the entire family was suddenly snatched away, it left a void virtually impossible to fill. They still missed her terribly.

If these circumstances were not already bad enough, their worries had been multiplied. When Maysel's disappearance was first acknowledged, Lela was panic-stricken, in shock, distraught, devastated and heartbroken. In the beginning, they were convinced, (and hoped and prayed) that Frank would tire of the responsibility of a five-year-old and return her to her mother. That never happened.

Shortly after Christmas, Lela began to fail. Unable to maintain her house, the Pittsenbargers closed Lela's house. They discarded most of her furniture and moved the things she would need into their home. She needed their care. Simple household chores became too much for her. Her parents began to notice a serious regression. Lela still could be brought to tears with just the mention of Maysel's name. She had become withdrawn from her surroundings, as well as reality. Often, she could be found holding Maysel's birthday photo, clutching it in her arms as if it was really Maysel. Lela was finally facing the cold-hard truth. Maysel was gone and the chances of ever seeing her again were slim . . . if not impossible. The force of this devastating reality was just too overwhelming for Lela and was much more than she could endure, mentally or physically.

Eating less and less as time went by, Lela was swiftly becoming thinner and thinner. Her parents begged her to eat, but she refused. Time after time, their efforts to persuade her to eat was aborted and Lela's health continued to decline. Far from the vibrant, happy, energetic, young lady she once was, Lela now spoke only when spoken to. Her only participation in any conversation would be "yes, or no, or maybe, or thank you." It seemed as though her mind was shutting down as well as her body. She spent most of her time in a darkened room, sitting in a chair, or in a bed. She refused to leave the house for any reason. Attending church had been Lela's passion, but no longer would she go. It wasn't that she had lost her faith in God. Her emotional, mental, and physical condition was steadily deteriorating. In spite of everything and everybody's willingness to help, there was nothing that could be done to help her.

It was February, 1930 and very little was known about breakdowns of any kind, mental, emotional or physical. Lela's entire being had been consumed by deep, serious depression. Valentine's Day arrived. It is believed that *this* was the day that finally pushed Lela over the edge. The very thought of having to live the rest of her life without seeing her sweetheart (Maysel) was just too powerful and overwhelming for Lela. Her weakened condition left her with little or no strength to fight it. This day was the final blow. Normally weighing one hundred, forty pounds, she now weighed a mere ninety-three pounds. Sinking farther and farther into the depths of despair, Lela apparently was losing her will to live. She was very much aware that her condition was causing her parents great stress and pain, but she just couldn't help herself. She had given up.

The morning following Valentine's Day, Mama prepared breakfast for Lela and called her to the table as usual.

"Lela," Mama called. "Lela, breakfast is ready Honey. Come on and eat." No response came from the room where Lela was. "Lela, wake up Honey." Mama sang the phrase, trying to bring a little cheer into Lela's life. Still, there was no answer.

Papa got up from his hair at the table and went into Lela's room. Her frail, fragile body lay there motionless. She was lying on her side with her face toward the wall. Papa opened the shades and curtains, letting in some morning sunlight.

"Lela," He said gently. "Honey, ain't ya gonna

come in here and eat with us? No response. "Baby, please get up and come on now." He begged. Still there was no answer from Lela. Moving himself around the bed to see her face, Papa suspected something was not quite normal. He knew Lela had been sick, but he had never seen her like this. With a tear in his eye, and very alarmed, he quickly left the room in search of Mama. Moments later, he and Mama were back in the room. Mama walked around the side of the bed to investigate and assess Lela's condition. A look of great disappointment and sorrow came over Mama's face. She knew this was not good. Taking Lela's hand, Mama tried desperately to communicate with her.

"Lela." She spoke her name. Mama's voice was almost a whisper. The heaviness on Mama's chest from what she saw almost made her breathing impossible. She looked very closely at her daughter. Lela just stared at the wall, said nothing and remained lifeless. Seeming to focus on nothing, Lela continued to stare straight ahead, not aware of anything around her. She was completely withdrawn.

"Papa, go get her some water to drink." Mama was emotional by now and feeling helpless. "Even if she won't eat, maybe she'll drink." Mama said as tears came. Mama was fearful that Lela's life would soon end if some miracle did not occur.

Almost immediately, Papa returned with a glass of water. Mama raised Lela's head and lifted the glass to her dry parched mouth. She succeeded in getting a small amount of the water into Lela's mouth. They attempted several times to communicate with Lela, but failed. Not knowing what more to do, they left the room. They could no longer ignore the fact that Lela was in bad need of a doctor.

For the next three weeks, Lela was a complete invalid and required constant and most personal care from Mama and Papa. Since the day after Valentine's Day, she had remained in bed. Her health had rapidly declined. Still unresponsive and weighing only about seventy-five to eighty pounds, her body showed no resemblance to Lela Pittsenbarger. That which was youthful and healthy, now was critically ill, looking like a very old woman and was dying. The small amount of flesh left on her back was being devoured by bedsores. Nearly half her hair had fallen out, and her teeth had become loose. Deteriorated to a mere skeleton she was lying there like a broken doll. If she opened her eyes at all, she just stared straight ahead and it was for just a brief moment, then she closed them again. She was so weak that opening her eyes required much too much effort, so she kept them shut. Lela had not spoken a word, had not eaten a bite of food, nor had she taken even one step. The limit of her consumption was small amounts of water given to her in a spoon, and she was refusing that. Mama had to practically force it down her throat.

Dr. Meadows was called in to see if he could offer help. Lifting her eyelid, looking into her mouth, taking her pulse and examining the condition of her body, he shook his head and looked at the Pittsenbargers.

"How long has she been like this? He asked.

"Between three or four weeks." Mama answered.

"She won't talk, eat, drink, won't even open her eyes anymore, and she looks awful. Look at her. Doc, I'm scared." She whispered, hoping Lela didn't hear her.

Doc Meadows guessed that if Lela didn't eat and take liquids soon, her fate would surely be death. Not much was known about clinical depression at that time, but he could tell from her condition that death was very near. She was severely dehydrated and suffered malnutrition. These were two deadly forces alone, without being accompanied by severe depression.

Standing at the door preparing to leave, Doc Meadows shook his head. "I'm sorry to tell you this." He said. "There's really nothing I can do. Survival depends totally on Lela. It's crucial. She must drink and eat and if she doesn't . . . I'm afraid two days will be a long life for her. From what I see, it doesn't look like that's going to happen." Avoiding the display of emotions that he expected to erupt, he shook their hands and quickly departed.

They had every right to believe that Lela was in a state of unconsciousness, but she wasn't. Lying there in her motionless state, she could hear everything being said around her. She heard the prayers of her parents as they cared for her, she could hear the dogs barking in the distance, she could hear Papa singing to her, and she also heard the statements made by Doc Meadows as he was leaving. Lela tried desperately to respond to them, but she was just too weak. It was as if her brain had canceled her ability to move, speak, eat, or drink. Now, she couldn't even open her eyes.

"I'm dying!" She thought. "Oh, God, please,

somebody help me!" Her mind cried out from deep inside her head, but no sound would come from her lips. "God! Please! God, where are you? Help me! Please, help me! If I can't see Maysel, then take me now. I don't want to live!" Her very soul screamed.

Suddenly, it was as if God Himself spoke to her deepest inner being. "Your child is not coming back to you. You must rise up from your bed, be healed and never give up your search for her. I promise, you will see her again, for I will raise up who I will and I will cast down who I will. I command you to rise up, for I will be your strength."

Lela could not determine if she had heard an audible voice, or if the voice she heard was telepathic. Immediately she felt a surge of strength run through her entire body. Still in a weakened state, she stirred and made a loud moaning noise. Her parents were in the other room. Looking at each other in total amazement, they rushed to her side. She made the sound again and her eyes opened for the first time in weeks. Leaning over Lela's body, Mama called her name. "Lela." She said, "Lela honey. It's Mama. We love you, baby. Please don't leave us!" She cried. "We're right here with you. Can you hear me, Lela? Waiting anxiously for a response, they stared at Lela's pitiful face, wanting just one sign of awareness. Lela managed to slowly shake her head, "yes."

Papa was out of the room in a flash and very quickly returned with water and soup. They began feeding Lela water with a spoon first and that would give them time to purée soup with a fork to make it almost liquid. She was eating and drinking for the first time in weeks. It was a very slow process, but she was eating. This was the most important factor. The first feeding took about two hours. They were so deeply thankful for their new hope. Almost a cup of soup and almost a cup of water . . . great! If they could keep a steady flow of soup and water going into her around the clock, they were certain that she would live. And they were right. Food, water, and love were the medicines needed to save her.

Each passing day brought Lela closer to recovery. Within a week, she was able to sit propped up in bed. Her eyes remained opened for almost normal periods of time. She was unable to hold objects, but she could move her arms and hands slightly. These were very promising signs. So pleased were they with her progress that they called Doc Meadows for a visit. Her improvement shocked him so much that he gasped in disbelief when he saw her. A huge smile lit up his face and he shouted, "Would you look at this!" His excitement brought a faint smile to Lela's face as she waved weakly at him. "It's amazing what tender love and care will do, now isn't it? He beamed. "Whatever you've been doing," he said, "Keep doing it. It's working." He whispered. Cutting his visit short, Mama and Papa escorted Doc Meadows out onto the porch. He turned to them and waved good-bye, still wearing a look of bewilderment on his face. He just couldn't believe it. The last time he had seen Lela, he would have bet big money that she would never have survived. "Hmm." He thought, "Miracles never cease. And, I just witnessed one."

Her long stay in bed had taken its toll. It took

Lela several weeks, but with her parents help, she was learning to walk again. She now was feeding herself. With little assistance, she could dress herself. She was beginning to talk more and more. It seemed that she was returning to her normal self. Lela still had a long way to go, but she was accepting visitors from the church. They seemed to cheer her up and they always said a prayer before leaving.

By early May, Lela had progressed so much that she was functioning very normally. Her appetite was normal, she was rapidly gaining her weight back and she had been going out of the house to attend church. The congregation was aware of the life-threatening experience she had just come through and they really felt blessed to witness a true, walking, living miracle.

May 6 would mark Maysel's birthday and some folks feared that Lela might regress. This sent a wave of fear through her family. Mama and Papa discussed it and decided it best for Lela visit Uncle Fred and his wife Lizzy. The couple lived at Cabin Creek near Charleston, West Virginia. The distance was rather far, but maybe she would be willing to spend the rest of the summer there. They planned on heavily suggesting this idea to Lela in hopes the she would be in agreement. The community had been buzzing with the news of Frank and Lela's "divorce" and of Lela's near-death experience. A vacation away from all of this (Mama and Papa thought) would do Lela a world of good.

Testing the waters, Mama made mention of the idea to Lela one evening at dinner. The idea was a

great one! Lela was excited and more than willing
to expand her existence, venture out and enjoy life a
little. Following a near-death experience and coming
to know how valuable life really is, she vowed never
to abuse God's gift of life again. Surviving her ordeal
had actually made her stronger in many ways. The one
thing that strengthened her most was God's promise
to her. At a time when she was waiting for death to
take her, He promised her that He would raise her
up, give her a second chance at life, grant her the
strength to search for Maysel, and that she would live
to see her child again. Now, all she needed to do was
to wait for God. She had faith that He would open
doors for her, make a way for her and place people in
her life to help her. "I don't stand in church and sing
'Standing on the promises of God' and not believe
it." She thought. Her faith in Him was stronger than
ever. God's time is not man's time and in His own
time, Lela knew in her heart the He would fulfill His
promise to her. Maybe this trip would be an opened
door. Either way, she must continue her search for
Maysel.

Chapter 18

May arrived and Maysel had been living in Laurel Branch Hollow for eight months. The cold and snow was gone and spring was in the air. Maysel had survived a very rough winter in the hollow and almost felt like a prisoner. John allowed her to go to the store with him if (and only if) she needed to be fitted for new bib overalls. She had been off the hill and down the hollow no more than three times since her arrival. Her life seemed reclusive and desolate. John was her only human contact and he wasn't home that much during the daytime. He was always gone "on business," but never failed to leave a list of assignments for Maysel, and these chores were to be completed by the time he returned. Poppy had changed so much since they moved into the hollow. At one time, (and Maysel could remember) he was a loving father and husband. No longer did he seem excited when he came home. No more candy treats, no more throwing her up over his head, no more telling her how much he loved her. Who *was* this stranger he had become? Who was the stranger living inside Poppy's body? Work, work, work, that's all he ever seemed to want of her. If she was not feeding the animals, gathering eggs, runnin' "shine," then she must be performing some other form of work. Unless John was giving her an order and another command, he had little to say to her. Maysel was terribly lonely and had no one with whom to talk to or play with. The only children she had met were the Varney children and Poppy had told her never to bother them. "Besides," he had said, "White kids don't play with colored kids." And that was that.

The horses had come in handy this spring. Poppy had used them to plow the soil so they could plant their crops for the season. There were many, many more fields of corn than anything else. His reason for this (if asked) was that he had to feed it to his horses and his hogs, which Mr. Varney was keeping for him. Of course, Maysel knew the real reason was that the corn was mostly used to run "shine."

The entire summer, Maysel ran "shine." Poppy bootlegged it and stashed the money back. Living like hermits was just exactly what John wanted. He had a good business going and some one to run it (labor free). Maysel could "shine" better than he, mainly because (thanks to him) she was more experienced.

John came home one afternoon and seemed to be concerned about Walter McCarty, a man who lived about three or four houses from them. He had died suddenly and tragically. Maysel had never seen any of the McCarty's. Associating with the neighbors was forbidden. Apparently, the McCarty's kept to themselves as well. Having visitors at the cabin was an absolute NO! NO! They might discover the "business."

John and Maysel went to feed their hogs at Mr. Varney's and while they were there, she overheard their conversation. Mr. McCarty was plagued with what they called "fits" (seizures). She gathered from the conversation that Mr. McCarty was at the creek letting his horse drink. While his horse was drinking, Mr. McCarty was overcome by one of these "fits." Convulsing and incoherent, he had fallen facedown into the creek and drowned. The creek was only about three inches deep. He was the father of six children ranging in age from five to fourteen years of age. They were three boys and three girls.

It was *mandatory* that all men in the hollow meet at the residence of a deceased person. If *any* man who lived in the hollow should neglect his duty to help with a death in the hollow, he would be dragged from his home in the middle of the night (sometime in the near future) and "flogged." Yes, beaten with a razor strap. No one wanted to face that penalty, so like all other men in the hollow, John rushed to the McCarty residence.

When death occurred in the hollow, the men built coffins of pine, placed the body in it and buried it in a hillside graveyard. If the deceased was male, his body was attended by the men of the hollow. If the deceased was female, her body was attended by women.

The two men said good-bye. John and Maysel made their way to the McCarty's so John could make an appearance and decide what his part would be in the funeral.

It was a lengthy walk, but Maysel was able to keep up with John, who seemed to be in a burry. I suppose his haste was accelerated with the notion that if a dead body wasn't buried within twenty-four hours from the time of death, (especially in the summertime) it would quickly begin to smell from decomposition. He needed to gather information concerning the funeral arrangements immediately, if he was to avoid being "flogged."

Knocking on the door of the McCarty residence, John was greeted by one of the neighbor women. There were several there. What John and Mr. Varney had discussed earlier about Mr. McCarty was true, and John was told that the men of the hollow had gathered in the barn to decide who would work on the coffin, who would dig the grave, and who would be assigned to attend the body. John paused before heading toward the barn and introduced Maysel to the women. They were strangers and Maysel was shy, but they managed to get through it. John instructed Maysel to remain on the porch until he returned from the barn. The porch looked a lot like theirs, (all the houses in the hollow resembled each other) so Maysel made her way to the far end of it and sat down. She could hear a lot of crying coming from within the house. Mrs. McCarty's voice was the most audible, but she could also hear the crying of children, which greatly disturbed her. Phrases such as, "we're gonna miss him so bad," and "what are we gonna do without him?" and "I can't believe he's really gone," were being spoken by different voices. Maysel was very upset with this entire affair. She had never given herself time to grieve the loss of her mother and grandparents, whom she had not seen for almost a year now. She knew how it felt to miss one of your parents. She sat there alone on the porch with her face in her lap and began to cry with them. She felt their pain as well as feeling her own.

She sensed someone looking at her. Raising her head slowly, she was eye to eye with a young lad whose face was also wet. His eyes were pooled and overflowing with tears. They just stared at each other for a moment. Neither really knew what to say to the other.

Finally, the lad wiped his eyes as if to be strong and said, "Who are *you*?

"My name is Maysel." She said.

"What are ya doin' here and why are *you* crying?" He asked.

"I'm with my Poppy. He's in the barn with the other men and he told me to wait for him here on the porch, and . . . I'm *not* crying." She stubbornly said.

"Yes you were. I saw ya." He said

"Did not."

"Did too. I know what I saw." He declared.

"Shut up," she demanded, "and just leave me alone." Maysel said.

"How come I ain't never seen you 'round here before? He asked.

"Cause I ain't never been 'round here before. We just moved up this holler early last fall." She explained. "What's your name?

"Name's Wannie." He said.

"Your name's about as different as mine." She

said.

"Yeah, it is. You never told me why you was cryin'. I guess I was cryin' 'cause my daddy died today. They'll probably bury him tomorrow and I'll never see him again. Not as long as I live." Wannie said sadly and with a far away look on his face.

"And, I probably won't ever see my Mommy again either. I ain't seen her for a long time. Poppy said Jesus came and took her with Him." Maysel said to him.

"Well, if Jesus came and took her, that means she's dead too." Wannie said.

"That's what I was afraid of. I guess that must be why I was cryin'. Everybody else was cryin' and it made me cry too." Maysel said. Changing the subject, Maysel asked, "How old are you?"

Wanting to sound older, Wannie said, "I'm a little over ten. How old are you?

"I'm almost seven." She lied. She was barely six.

"Do you go to school? Wannie asked.

"Nope," Maysel replied, and proudly announced, "Poppy said I don't *have* to go either."

"Well, we have to go and it starts again next month. I *hate* it, but I guess I'll go anyhow." Wannie remarked to her. "Mommy *makes* us go whether we want to or not." He said.

They continued small talk for the next few minutes and while they were doing so, Maysel took notice of Wannie. He looked stronger than ten. In a few years, his slender body would develop into a very muscular, virile, handsome young man. The

McCarty kids were much like the Varney's. They had to work hard. The survival of their families required it. Looking at his slender face, Maysel was compelled to stare at Wannie's eyes. Big, blue and framed by a thick row of the darkest, longest eyelashes Maysel had ever seen. They were beautiful as were his teeth. Big, white and straight, they seemed to gleam in the sun as he spoke.

"Are you comin' to the funeral tomorrow? Wannie asked as he observed her dark blonde hair, which had grown down to her shoulders by now. It had not been cut since her fifth birthday last year.

"I don't know," she answered, "I have to wait and see what Poppy says." She wanted to say yes, but had no way of knowing whether or not she could go. "I'd like to go. I've never been to a funeral before."

John came around the corner of the house. Putting his hand on Wannie's shoulder and shaking it gently, he said, "Now, which one are you? Poppy asked Wannie.

"I'm Wannie." He answered mannerly.

"Well, you're a fine lookin' young man. This is Maysel, my little girl." Poppy said as he put his hand on Maysel's shoulder.

"Can Maysel come to the funeral tomorrow, Mr. Brunty? Wannie wanted to know.

"Uuuuuh." Poppy said, thinking about it. "I don't see why not. If she wants to." He looked at Maysel to gather her thoughts. Maysel shook her head "yes." Poppy looked at Wannie and said, "Sure, why not." He figured that this could just be another learning experience for Maysel.

They said their good-byes and Poppy and Maysel
left. Poppy had some planning to do. He had agreed
to be a gravedigger. He was not good at wood work
and he was a single parent. Three hours of digging
would be more convenient. He used Maysel as an
excuse to be relieved of the responsibilities of other
deed, which would require more of his time. (How
convenient.)

The next day was a busy one. Several women
from the hollow had brought food to the McCarty
house and had attended to the needs of the family
while the men of the hollow busied themselves
preparing Mr. McCarty's body for burial. He had
died the previous afternoon, so he must be put to rest
early this afternoon. Embalming procedures were not
practiced and burying the dead within twenty-four
hours was of utmost importance.

The coffin, a long wooden box painted black, was
displayed in the front room. It was supported on each
end by a ladder-backed chair. Maysel had never seen
a coffin, a dead person, nor had attended a funeral.
The hollow people were poor. There were no floral
arrangements, only a small bouquet of flowers that
was placed in Mr. McCarty's hand.

Standing guard near the coffin with a broom and
a fly swatter was a male attendant. His responsibility
was to keep cats and flies away from the body. Cats
were known to attack bodies, chewing on them and
causing damage. Flies would lay eggs in the nostrils
and ears, which produced maggots in a matter of a
few hours. *This* was an important job.

People wandered in and out the house all morning

long viewing Mr. McCarty's body and trying to be of comfort to the family. Paying their respects to the family, they all walked around whispering to each other as if they didn't want to disturb Mr. McCarty. Maysel recognized very few people, so she tried to blend into the crowd. Once in a while, somebody might notice and ask her who she was. Then Maysel would to explain her presence.

At one o'clock, the family gathered in the front room of the house. All others congregated on the front porch or out in the yard. The windows were left open so everyone outside could hear the funeral service. The schoolhouse was used for these functions only if the weather was rainy or cold. Other than that, funeral services were usually conducted at the home of the deceased.

There seemed to be a great respect for the Bible, God and religion. Neighbors often met at each others homes for prayer meetings, but not all of them participated, however, *all* the families were God-fearing and lived by the Golden Rule. Ordained ministers were not plentiful and self-proclaimed, God-called ministers preached for them. One such minister officiated Mr. McCarty's funeral services.

When the minister went to stand at the head of the coffin, everyone became silent. He read a passage from the Bible and added, "It is appointed unto man once to die, and after that, the judgment. It is most unfortunate that Jesus has come to claim another one of His children, Mr. McCarty. He will be sadly missed by his family as well as his friends. If," he said, "*you* have not prayed the prayer of repentance and have not accepted Jesus Christ as your personal Savior, then when it comes your time to go, unlike Brother McCarty, *you* will *not* go to Heaven with Him. Instead, you will be eternally lost and doomed to the pits of Hell!" He proclaimed loudly, (After all that whispering.) "My prayer and condolences are with this family, but their loss is Heaven's gain. Now, with every head bowed, we shall recite the Lord's Prayer." He led them in prayer. Immediately a quartet with guitars and stringed instruments sang a beautiful song, "Just a Rose Will Do." After that, he asked everyone to join together in singing a chorus of "Amazing Grace."

While the congregation was singing, he nodded his head to a group of men who immediately came forward. The family was ushered to the outside of the house. The coffin lid was fitted into place and tacked down with a hammer. A receiving line had formed in the yard to receive the grieving family. Six men carried the pine box containing Mr. McCarty's body out of the house and loaded it onto a waiting wagon. The family (first behind the wagon) and congregation followed the wagon to the cemetery, walking behind it. Maysel could not take her eyes off Wannie who was the only friend she had since coming here. One thing they had in common was that they both had lost a parent. She hoped their friendship would grow.

The cemetery was located high on a hill, which made pulling the wagon more difficult for the horses. Maysel had never witnessed anything like this before. It was quite an experience for her and she could not quite grasp the meaning of it all.

Finally there, Maysel noticed three ropes about twenty feet long. Each was stretched out parallel to each other at the gravesite. As family and friends gathered near the grave, the six men lifted the coffin down from the wagon and set it down on top of the ropes. Each man took his place and grasped the end of a rope. On cue, they lifted the ropes (with the coffin on them) and very carefully lowered the coffin into the deep cavity. Once it was in place, the ropes were removed and the service was continued.

The minister read a passage or two from the Bible and said, "Ashes to ashes and dust to dust. We commend our brother Walter McCarty back to the mother dust in the name of the Father, (he threw a flower into the grave) and of the Son, (he threw another flower into the grave) and of the Holy Ghost (he threw another flower into the grave). Turning to the family and friends, he said, "May God's spirit comfort you in this time of sorrow and may you find healing for your broken hearts in Him. May you find strength in Christ." Several men stayed behind to fill in the grave while everyone left the cemetery to return to their homes.

Maysel and Wannie watched each other the whole time. A long-lasting friendship was forming. Since affection was lacking in both their lives and neither of them received much attention from their parents, they channeled these energies toward each other. They were both young and innocent. This friendship would dramatically affect the future of both children. They had no way of knowing just how much.

Walking down the hill from the cemetery, Maysel

became very upset, but she could not discuss her confusion with anyone.

"So," she thought, "is this what Jesus does when he 'claims' one of His own? He puts you in a box, nails the lid shut, lowers you into a big hole and covers you with dirt! My God! None of this makes sense! Is this how He 'claimed' my mommy? With these thoughts, Maysel's breath became shorter, her head was spinning, her heart was racing and seemed like it would explode. Maysel was experiencing a major panic attack and with the exception of Wannie, she had no one to help her with it. She sat down on the ground, put her head between her knees and waited for this "spell" to wear off. Wannie never left her side until she was able to continue their journey off the hill. Oh, how much she appreciated him. He was someone who was much kinder to her than her own father. Amazing.

Chapter 19

*U*nknown to Lela, Fred and Lizzy had visited several times while she was sick and bedfast. During their visits, it had been discussed with her parents and it was agreed that she should spend the remainder of the summer with them in Cabin Creek. That is, if she survived. The invitation was open and it was decided that Lela could stay with them as long as she wished. Uncle Fred and Aunt Lizzy loved Lela as if she were their own.

Walking around as if on pins and needles, Mama put forth every effort to keep Lela's excitement levels high and her mind off Maysel's up and coming birthday. Nina prayed that Lela would allow nothing to dampen her spirits about staying with Uncle Fred and Aunt Lizzy for a while.

The price of a new wardrobe for Lela was not financially possible, so Nina spent a lot of her time altering Lela's old clothes to better fit her new, slender figure. Still too lean, Lela's clothes hung on her small frame like sacks. Her mother was very handy with a needle and thread, as were several of the churchwomen. Preparing Lela for her trip became a group effort. The Pittsenbargers were loved by their church family. These people were more than willing to do anything possible to help them through these very troubled times. After all, a miracle had occurred in their church and their faith was running high. Being separated from Lela for the rest of the summer didn't make them happy, but they had to consider the ordeal that she and her family had been through during the past few months. They wished her well.

Lela's divorce had become "old news" to the folks in the community and they had become adjusted to the fact that Lela was no longer married and that John was no longer a part of her life. No matter what the details were, Lela was not responsible for what had happened in her life and they accepted her innocence in the matter with a forgiving spirit. They still admired Lela for her virtues as a Christian and as a lady. Frank's having another wife had placed Lela in a very unusual position. *He* had failed, not Lela. He had committed adultery and therefore, Lela had every right to "put him away" (get a divorce; put him out of her life). As if that wasn't enough, he had taken and disappeared with her only child, nearly causing Lela her life. What a cruel and inhumane thing for even him to do. Divine intervention brought on by the prayers of these incredible people and their faith in God was to be credited for Lela's miraculous recovery. Her friends and family were thrilled that God had answered their prayers and Lela had survived.

Lela's clothes were ready and everyone was outside the small residence waiting to see her off.

Virtually, everyone who knew the Pittsenbargers was present. This day was considered a tremendous victory, not only for Lela, but also for those who loved her. Each person was happy to have been instrumental (no matter how small) in Lela's rise to good health. Lela checked to make certain she would leave nothing behind. Suddenly, she darted back into the house and returned with Maysel's photo. A silence fell and every eye was on Lela. They were looking for any sign of emotion, but found none. Her family and friends had become so fixated on her, and so worried about her emotional well being that they didn't want to give her the slightest opportunity to regress back into the life-threatening situation, which consumed her life a few weeks ago. She remained radiant, smiling and happy. Nothing suggested regression. Carefully placing the photo between two garments so it would not be broken, Lela turned her attention to her friends, made her farewells, waving to them as she watched their images seem to grow smaller and smaller until they were no longer visible. Oh, how much she loved these people and, of course, the feelings were mutual. The summer would pass quickly and they would be reunited again soon. Lela had plans to write them letters and keep in touch.

The ride from her home in Greenbrier County to Cabin Creek was exhausting. Lasting about four hours, Lela, Fred and Lizzy had talked about everything and everyone that they knew and had sung just about every song that they knew. This helped time to pass faster.

Darkness had fallen and Lela could hardly wait

to drop into bed for a much-needed rest. She was so tired that she failed to notice the new curtains and rugs in Fred and Lizzy's house until she awoke the next morning and commented on them. Seeing Lela troop to the breakfast table with a big appetite was an exciting and happy sight for Fred and Lizzy. A huge country breakfast with all the trimmings had been prepared for Lela. Lizzy was elated when her home-cooked meal was devoured by the frail and recovering houseguest.

The last of the breakfast dishes were washed and put away. Everyone was dressed and ready for the day. They planned on taking Lela into town to show her off. They also wanted to introduce her to some of their friends and acquaintances. Fred and Lizzy were financially better off than most of her relatives, so they treated Lela to a lot of things that were not affordable at home. They window shopped, looked at fashions, bought candy from the candy store, ate ice cream and just plain enjoyed the beautiful day by taking in some sights of the small town. Lela was not from a small "town." She was from a rural community, so this was a pretty big thing for her.

Aunt Lizzy was in her early fifties and had an absolutely astonishing ability to speak for hours at a time without stopping to take a breath. She never shut up. Seemingly, she could tell whole stories without so much as a pause, but in spite of this gift of gab, she was a very good, kind, caring and loving person. Maybe her "gift" would be instrumental in keeping Lela's mind off her own life for a few weeks. It did, however, make her ears tired. Poor Fred, on the other hand was a little more relaxed. He never seemed to get in a hurry or loose his temper. He talked very little and was such a sweetheart. How he put up with Lizzy's chatter day in and day out was a mystery to Lela, but Lizzy was his world and he really loved her. She silently wished to find a good, kind, gentle-natured man like Fred someday. Fred and Lizzy seemed to be a perfect match.

Her time was completely occupied. Since Lela's arrival in Cabin Creek, her days had been pre-planned by Fred and Lizzy, who were determined to fill her time with happy and pleasant experiences: church socials, visits into town, walks by the river, a barn dance, (oops, dancing was a sin back home). Lela even saw her first automobiles drive through town while she was there. This was so exciting! One couple even took her for a ride in one. She couldn't wait to tell her friends back home about that. They had succeeded in keeping her busy, but the thing she liked most was their church. It had an organ (her church did not) and someone played it for the congregation. Lela loved it. Three more weeks would end the summer visit and Lela would return home to her parents.

Chapter 20

*H*aving only two weeks left before returning home, Lela wanted to make the best of it. They set out on a trip to the big city. The number of stores seemed endless and they spent most of the day looking through them. Wow! Lela had never seen anything like Charleston, West Virginia. The state capitol seemed larger than life. Her mind could not comprehend its magnitude. There were many automobiles and the streets were filled with people going in and out of the numerous stores and business places. Lela really liked all the action. She had never seen so many people in one place. They seemed to swarm like colonies of ants on an anthill. With their arms full of purchases, the shoppers hurried along appearing to be completely oblivious to anyone else on the streets. Money was very scarce in her world and she was quiet overwhelmed by all of this spending. This exchange of huge amounts of money in one place was incomprehensible to her. It was truly another world that had a tiring effect on Lela, but she was having such a good time that she ignored the fatigue. Her summer visit would soon be over, so she pushed herself to enjoy the rest of it. Fred and Lizzy had been very attentive to Lela during her visit and she didn't want them to remotely think that she was not having a wonderful time. They had been on a mission to keep Lela's mind busy and occupied during her stay with them. One could say Lela had been given the "royal" treatment.

Turning to enter the door of a large hardware store, the trio was in a hurry to let Fred shop for a couple of tools that he was in need of. Lela was walking in front of them and just as she opened the door to enter, a frightened cat raced between her feet quickly exiting the building. In a state of surprise, Lela's feet began to uncontrollably dance from one to the other and during her "dance" one of her feet came down onto one of the cat's feet. The scream emitted by the cat was deafening. In an effort to put a lot more distance between itself and the door that had kept it prisoner, the cat shrieked and bolted down the street. Projecting a startled look, Lela held both hands on her chest, she was breathing hard and her eyes were wide open as if she would surely faint and all she could say was, "Oh . . . oh . . . oh"

The next shopper coming out of the store couldn't help but encounter this event. Placing his hand on Lela's shoulder to help her regain her balance, he inquired if she was all right. He even followed them inside the store to be certain. There was a brief conversation between the four, and introductions were made. Following that, Fred excused himself to search for his needed tools and Lizzy decided to browse, leaving the stranger and Lela alone. Two benches happened to be by the door. They sat down on them and made small talk about what had just occurred, laughing about it as they talked.

Lela finally composed herself and took a moment to catch her breath. Looking up, she got a glimpse of the man who was being so kind and considerate to her. Jack Trout had rich brown hair that was just beginning to gray along his temples. He kept it combed and trimmed with the discipline one might expect from an air force veteran. Jack's bright blue eyes were topped by a pair of graceful eyebrows and possessed a "Santa Claus" twinkle. They projected a look of kindness that added to his charm. Small wrinkles had begun to form from the corners of his mouth and beside his eyes, giving his lean, sharp face more character. She guessed him to stand about six feet, one inch in height. He wasn't fat, but well built. The man was strong, yet he seemed gentle and sensitive, which led Lela to view him as a gentle giant. His clothes were clean, as was his person, and he displayed many good qualities such as honesty, kindness and caring. All of this and he appeared to be about her age.

They settled down from all the excitement and Jack spoke. "What's your name?

"Lela Ad . . . uh, Pittsenbarger." She stammered.

"Are you from 'round here, or just visiting? He inquired.

"I've been visiting my aunt and uncle all summer, but I going back to Greenbrier County in two weeks." She explained.

"I'm Jack Trout." He said, extending his hand.

They shook hands and continued their conversation. There was an instant attraction, but Lela couldn't even think about that at this time, not after the ordeal she had just came through with Frank Adams.

"Are you married? Jack asked.

"No, are you?" Lela asked.

"No. I just never thought about it yet.

"Where are you from?" Lela wanted to know.

"At the moment, I live near here, but I go where ever my jobs lead me. I've worked in the coalmines and sawmills most recently. I can move with no trouble since I'm not married." He offered. "Hey, I've got tickets to the circus tonight. Would you like to go with me? One of my good friends was supposed to go with me, but now he can't go. No use wasting the tickets and besides you'd be doing me a favor." He smiled kindly at her.

Lela, now becoming uncomfortable, looked around for any sign of Lizzy or Fred. There was Lizzy standing at the end of the aisle. Lela spoke her name and Lizzy joined them. "Aunt Lizzy, this nice young man has invited me to go to the circus with him tonight. What do you think? Lela would accept, only with Lizzy's approval.

Lizzy, being a good judge of character looked at Jack and said, "I think that's just what the doctor ordered. A fun time out on the town with a young man would do you a world of good Lela. Jack seems to be a mannerly young gentleman. I think he'll show you a real good time, go on!" There, Lela had Lizzy's blessings, but she had mixed feelings. Why not go? She had been a recluse and had experienced far too many bad things to deprive herself a trip to the circus. In fact, Lela had never seen a circus. The performers dressed scantily and some of her friends thought it sinful to observe them doing their feats in such revealing clothes. "Who cares," Lela thought, "I'm going anyway." So, she accepted his gracious invitation and they made plans for this "*date*"? Is this a *date*? No, it's just a trip to the circus. Lela wasn't ready to *date* yet.

Jack excused himself. As he left the store and with his back to Lela, a big grin crossed his face. His lifestyle prohibited him from dating very much, but this would have to take priority over work. There was something very special about this young woman. It was a rare occasion for Jack to ask for a date with just one meeting, but he could not help himself. He just had to ask her out and he could hardly contain his excitement when she said, "Yes."

The circus was to begin at 6:00 pm. Fred and Lizzy had insisted on delivering Lela to the circus grounds. Thinking of Maysel's abduction when she planned on attending the fair made their hearts skip beats. Dear God! They couldn't go through that again, but Lela *must* continue her life. *Fear* should no longer be her companion. They hoped this evening would help Lela begin to dissolve that negative emotion.

Lela had never witnessed such excitement and noise. The tent for the big top was huge and sat in the center of the festivities, surrounded by circus cars, wagons, venders, etc. Crowds of people like none she had ever seen was walking between the cages of animals outside the massive tent. Loud music filled the air and the voices of hundreds of spectators were almost overwhelming. The smell of food and refreshments made Lela hungry. Adding to the curiosity of this event were strange-looking carnies. They were busy going in and out and around the cages and cars.

Lela, Lizzy, and Fred were to meet Jack near the ticket booth at the entrance to the circus. Standing there enjoying all the sights, sounds and smells, they searched the crowd for Jack. Lela spotted him first. Waving her arms to attract his attention, she lured Jack over to where they were standing. Producing the tickets and greeting everyone with a gentle hug Jack could not hide his interest. Fred and Lizzy announced that they would meet them at this same place following the circus in about two hours. Before leaving, they watched Jack and Lela disappear into the big tent.

As they entered, Jack took a quick look around to find the best available seats. His eyes fell on two good seats and he nudged Lela toward them. They rushed over and seated themselves. Jack, being ever a gentleman, asked Lela to save his seat while he went to get some popcorn and lemonade for them to enjoy during the show. While he was gone, Lela couldn't help gawking at all the sights. Hilarious clowns were running around in crazy-looking costumes and make-up. One of them had a monkey on his shoulder that was performing tricks. Carnies were busy checking the trapezes, tight ropes, nets and safety features of the big top. Others were busy selling popcorn and lemonade. The band consisted mostly of a huge organ accompanied by a drummer. It was playing pre-show music while the spectators were being seated. Lela particularly liked the marches and tapped her foot in merriment.

Jack returned just as the ringmaster was being introduced with a drum roll. Hurray! It's show time! Jack had seen the circus many times. He enjoyed it, but today, Lela was the center of his attention. Too interested in the show to notice, Lela didn't see that Jack was staring at her. He was thrilled that she was having such a good time. Lela never took her eyes off the performers and Jack never took his eyes off Lela.

The show ended and a flood of people began leaving the tent. Jack suggested that they let some of them leave before they attempted to exit.

"What did ya think of that? Jack asked with a big grin on his face. He already knew the answer to that question. He had seen it on her face throughout the show.

"Wow!" Lela said in amazement, "I've never seen anything quite like that before. I loved it! Wait'll I tell everybody about this when I get back home. They'll all be jealous"

"That's two weeks from today, right? Jack asked.

"Yes. I'm afraid I'm about to wear out my welcome here with Uncle Fred and Aunt Lizzy. They have shown me such a good time, but all good things must come to an end. They really cannot afford to spend any more of their time, money and effort on me. They're absolute dolls, both of them. I declare, they have kept me so busy I'm sure I'll have to rest for two weeks when I do get back home. I've had all of that from them, and now this great evening from you. How lucky can one girl be? She was beaming as she spoke.

"If you just have two more weeks in the Charleston area, can I see more of you while you're here? Jack inquired.

"I don't know yet. I'll let you know when we meet up with my aunt and uncle. I wouldn't want to make a decision that could possibly offend them. They are so good to me. What do you have in mind? Lela asked.

"Wednesday evening, there's a blue grass band playing near the capitol building. I'd love for you to go with me. Do you like blue grass?

"I like Christian music." She said.

"I do too. They play some Christian music. I just know you'll love it." He said trying to encourage her to go. "If you don't want to do that, then maybe we can just eat ice cream, go for a walk and just talk. I'd like to know more about you." He confided.

"There's not that much to know and besides, it could be very boring." She said as she turned her head while keeping her eyes on him.

"Let me be the judge of that." He said as he rose from his seat and directed her out of the tent.

The couple made their way toward the designated meeting place. Fred and Lizzy were standing in the same place as they were when Jack and Lela had last seen them. It was as though they had never left that spot. A look of excitement and awe was on

Lela's face and Lizzy could tell that the evening had been a tremendous success. This brought a smile of satisfaction to her face.

"Aunt Lizzy, may I speak to you in private? Lela asked as she excused herself and walked away with Lizzy.

"Jack wants me to go with him to hear a blue grass band Wednesday evening. It don't matter to me if you tell me not to, but I need your approval, or I'm not going." Lela said firmly.

"Lela, you are twenty-six years old and can make your own decisions. Do you want to go? Then go. If you don't, then don't go. It's that simple. Whatever you decide to do, Fred and I will support you and help you any way we can. We love you and want you to be happy." Lizzy said motherly.

"Well . . . he is nice. I don't know Aunt Lizzy. I do like him though. What to do? What to do? Are you sure it's O.K? She needed assurance.

"Go on Lela. I think he's good company. He seems very nice and all. If you don't want to see him after Wednesday, you can simply not see him anymore. You're going home in two weeks, remember? That'll put a few miles between the two of you and you won't have to be bothered with him if you don't want to be. It's just a music show. Go on for goodness sake." Lizzy coaxed.

The two women walked to where they had left Jack and Fred moments ago. Lela looked at Jack and said, "I'll be happy to go with you Wednesday evening. The arrangements will have to be the same. My uncle and aunt will bring me and they will take me back home with them."

"That's alright with me, whatever you say." He said. He couldn't believe she was agreeing to see him again. Could this work out for him? Is the woman of his dreams obtainable? Time would tell.

The next four days went by like a snail crossing a very wide road. Jack practically counted the minutes as they ticked by. So anxious for Wednesday night to arrive, he had difficulty sleeping and his mind was saturated with Lela's face. He had never felt like this about any other woman in his life. This just had to work out. That's all there was to it.

Escorted by Fred and Lizzy, Lela arrived at the musical performance. She had worn leggings to prevent bugs from biting her legs and, although it was summer, she wore long sleeves for the same reason. The couple would reunite with Fred and Lizzy three hours later. A nice crowd was gathering in front of a stage, which had been built for the musicians. Benches had been set up in theatre fashion and Jack and Lela sat down on one of them near the back. The audience clapped their hands and stomped their feet to the first few numbers played by the band. Lela thought the music and singing was great. People were allowed to dance if they wanted to, but Lela didn't dance and neither did Jack, so they just sat there enjoying the music and observing the merriment of others. Too shy to dance in public they may have been a little envious of those who weren't.

Jack slipped his hand over Lela's at one point during the evening and noticed that she did not retract or move it away from his. "Oh, my God." He thought, "This is a good sign. Could it be that she may like me too?

The music was over long before Fred and Lizzy were to return, so they took a walk. Jack wanted to know as much about Lela as he could possibly learn. Lela at first was skeptical and felt uncomfortable discussing her personal life with someone she just met four days prior. She discovered that Jack had never been married, had no children, was a very hard worker and loved family life. These were all good qualities. He had a flawless record. On the other hand, she was a divorced woman in the late 1920's and was considered "damaged goods." And, she was the mother of a child. How could she begin to tell him about Maysel? These facts alone would send any potential beau running swiftly in the opposite direction. Oh, well, she was who she was and she is who she is. Jack kept insisting that she tell him about herself. He had emphasized his story to be a very short and boring one.

Lela thought for a moment and said, "Do you really want to know all that. Some of it isn't very pretty, and you may not like me very much if you know my story."

"I'll risk it." He said.

"Well, I have nothing to lose and you will know sooner or later, so I'll tell you about myself." She took a deep breath and began telling Jack the story of being married to Frank, having Maysel, divorcing Frank, Maysel being stolen, having a break down, miraculously surviving it, and brought him up to the moment they were now sharing. Jack had asked her questions as she related her story.

"There, now just tell me to get lost and I don't blame you if you do. Nobody wants a divorced woman with a child." She said.

"None of that matters to me." He said kindly. "There's only one thing about all of this that bothers me." He looked at her with compassion in his eyes, took her hands in his and asked, "Where *is* your little girl?"

"I don't know. She's been missing for more than a year now." She said sadly as tears filled her eyes. "We've heard nothing."

He realized how painful this subject was for her and tried to comfort her by explaining that none of it was her fault. Frank was to blame for the entire painful mess. Then, Jack changed the subject to talk about the weather.

If they were not waiting for Fred and Lizzy when they returned to pick her up, Lela felt sure a reprimand would be in order. She didn't want that, so they hurried to their designated meeting spot.

While they waited for her uncle and aunt, Jack asked if he could see her again. Lela was a little surprised. The only thing she knew to do was to invite him to church Sunday morning and maybe they could visit Sunday afternoon. Jack agreed to the idea and promised to see her in church. And, he did.

Feeling right at home, happy and comfortable, Jack sat proudly by Lela in the House of God the next Sunday morning. Although he was tempted, he never offered to hold her hand. Lela appreciated his respectful spirit and found herself becoming more and more attracted to him. "I've only been divorced a year." She thought. "Is it too soon to have these feelings? After living through the past year, Lela felt that every day was a gift from God and she had no intentions of wasting precious life over silly notions. What will be, will be. God has a plan and far be it from her to interrupt it.

The next week and a half passed as if it was a feather in the wind. Lela and Jack had become more and more fond of each other as a result of their frequent visits and outings. Although they knew from the beginning that she would leave Cabin Creek and return home, they anticipated her departure with high anxiety. Jack was almost certain that Lela was the woman for him and Lela had a very strong attraction to Jack. She also felt a little guilty about having these feelings. She had only been separated from Frank for a little more than one year. Being a proper lady, Lela knew that if their relationship should blossom into a romance that it would be a *very* long time before she would *ever* marry again. Considering the series of events in her recent life, it might be impossible for Jack (or anyone else) to win her trust. Frank had caused serious damage in that area and it just might be irreparable. Only time would tell.

In a tizzy of excitement and stress, Fred, Lizzy and Lela set out for Greenbrier County. Fred and Lizzy had become accustomed to Lela's presence in their home. She had brought a little more life to their lives and they would miss her greatly. It was a Monday morning and a workday for Jack, which prevented him from seeing them off. That was alright. It would have been too sad for Jack and Lela to watch each other disappear from the other's sight. Jack was raring to go to another level in their relationship, but because of many factors, Lela was in denial and a slower pace suited her better. With enough miles between them, and if she ignored her feelings for Jack long enough, she thought surely they would pass. She was wrong.

Chapter 21

The summer was over and the tell-tale signs of fall were beginning to appear. The evenings were getting much cooler, the mornings were brisk and the days were glorious. A few leaves had begun to change colors. Temperatures were perfect and sparked an un-explained level of energy in the children. Most of the summer's hard, long work was over and just the "puttin' up" of fodder, corn and vegetables for the winter was the only "real" demand facing Maysel. Lately, she had a little more time to play.

Poppy was now leaving her alone for more extended periods of time. After all, a man needed the company of women didn't he? Oh yeah, far be it from John Brunty (alias, Frank Adams) to deny himself the attention of a women (or any other luxury) for very long. Some of his lady friends had recently been showing up at the cabin, even to stay as long as two weeks. According to John, Maysel was just a little girl and needed a female role model to teach her how to be a young lady. This false pretense was a load of crap! Whenever a "lady" friend came for a long visit, Maysel was told, "This is your new mother-

in-law. Be nice to her, and make yourself scarce."
The truth of the matter is that during "mother-in-
law's" stay, Maysel had to sleep on a mattress made
of sacks stuffed with dry leaves and straw-outside on
the ground, under a tree. Alone! A six and a half year-
old little girl isolated, in the dark, in the woods, and
cold! John Brunty was a selfish, uncaring bastard!

Retiring to her outside bed on such nights, Maysel
could hear giggling, laughing, moaning and groaning
coming from within the cabin located just a few yards
away from her bristly, make-shift bed. Innocence
prevented her from knowing what prompted those
sounds, but she wondered why she could not join in
the fun. She too would love to laugh and giggle, but
there was no one to laugh and giggle with.

In the darkness, she often wondered why Jesus
had taken her mother, why her father treated her so
unfairly, why she had to have a "mother-in-law,"
why she could not wear dresses, why was she made
to feel as though she was somehow "lower" than
everyone else? She would never find answers to these
questions. Not now, not ever, because these answers
did not exist. Still, in spite of everything connected
with her situation, she longed for the gentle touch
of her mother's hand, the smell of her mother, the
kindness of her grandparent's love, the father John
once was, and for the life she knew before being
taken to the hollow. Those were becoming distant
memories–memories that she often re-lived and revisited. Her dreary life could not prevent her from
dreaming.

On these nights of isolation and rejection,

Maysel often lay in the stillness of the country air listening to the crickets and sounds of other critters while she waited for sleep to overcome her and take her to a more peaceful, happier place . . . a place where people were kinder to her . . . a place where she was not treated like some annoying stray dog. She was often referred to as "that little bastard" by some of the hollow neighbors. John was usually late getting home from bootlegging his "shine," and was unconcerned about meals for Maysel. Hungry, she often found herself sitting in the threshold of neighbors' doors watching their families eat supper. Most of them never offered to share their food with her and just continued to eat as if she were not sitting there. Because of these unforgivable actions, deep-seated resentment built up inside Maysel . . . resentment so powerful that it bordered on hatred. Yet, she was always happy when a family member would offer her a biscuit with some apple butter on it . . . a real treat for her. If she was not successful in begging food from a neighbor, she could always count on Wannie McCarty, (her new-found friend) to bring her a bite to eat. She never received food two days in a row from the same family. They feared she would come to expect a hand-out every day and they were not about to raise John Brunty's kid for him. She did, however, make friends with some of the children who would slip her some food once in a while. For that, she was forever grateful. Maysel was tough, and becoming tougher. She was a survivor and concluded that life would always be a battleground for her . . . and she was right.

The noise of the first day of school was barely tolerable. Excitement filled the entire area where the children of the hollow were assembling and their voices echoed loud and clear. Education was not very good, but at least they would learn the three R's (reading, writing and arithmetic). The one-room school house accommodated grades one through eight, often doubled as a church and was even used for community gatherings.

A very nice, kind, and compassionate woman, Mrs. Hagerman was the only teacher for the school. Her very presence demanded the children's attention and respect. With a switch hanging in the corner of the room, she would not hesitate using it on an offensive student with the vengeance of a slave taskmaster. No one wanted to be the example for the year, so behavior was not a problem in her class room. Teachers had the authority to deliver punishment as severely as they desired and they were never challenged by any parent or authorities. School teachers at that time were respected as highly as policemen or clergy. Yep, if you were in trouble at school, then you were in deeper trouble at home when your parents discovered it.

Ringing the bell was considered a very special privilege by the students. Exercising this privilege was Albert Aliff. He strutted up to the bell and started pulling the rope. The bell sent loud ringing sounds that could be heard from far and wide throughout the hollow. Ringing it 15 times meant that school was to begin immediately and for all students to find a seat and quietly wait for Mrs. Hagerman to begin the day's learning.

Mrs. Hagerman stood up and a silence filled the room. "This is the first day of school and I will assign you your seats. As I call your name and point to a seat, I want you to get in it. This will be your permanent seat for the remainder of the school term, unless I move you. Is that clear?"

In unison, the class replied, "Yes Mrs. Hagerman."

"Thank you. Now, are all the school-age children from the hollow present?"

Wannie McCarty quickly raised his hand.

"Yes, Wannie what is it?"

"John Brunty has a little girl and he says that she don't have to go to school and if she don't have to go, then I don't have to go neither."

"Really? When did he come back to live here?"

"Last August! And she's six and a half too! That's old enough to have to go ain't it Mrs. Hagerman? Ain't it? "

"Yes, I believe it is and I need you to do me a favor, Wannie. Please deliver a note to Mr. Brunty for me this evening after school." She said firmly.

"Yes Ma'am. I'll do that for you this evening." Wannie replied. He was very eager to please Mrs. Hagerman and make Maysel go to school too. If he had to go to school, then she did too!

Hurray! School was out and Wannie's feet could not move fast enough to carry him to the head of the hollow to deliver the note from Mrs. Hagerman. If Maysel thought for a minute that she was gonna be excused from attending school, she had another thing coming.

Arriving on the porch with great leaps and bounds, Wannie rapped on the door of the cabin. The door opened and John Brunty coldly ask him what he wanted. Wannie handed him Mrs. Hagerman's note and shyly waited to see John's response. A look of disgust quickly came over John's face. He gritted his teeth and spit a load of tobacco juice from his mouth several feet over the edge of the porch. "We don't have to do a damn thing if we don't want to." He mumbled under his breath. Wannie could see that John was not happy with the contents of the note, so he excused himself and left the porch with the same level of energy that he had displayed on his arrival.

Mrs. Hagerman brought school to order and began roll call. She had added Maysel's name to the roll book the night before with the confidence that Maysel would answer the next morning. That did not happen. She called Maysel's name and the only response she received was Wannie McCarty declaring that he had in fact delivered her note immediately after school and also that Mr. Brunty had said that they didn't have to do nothing if they didn't want to.

She frowned and a look of determination registered on Mrs. Hagerman's face. She raised one eye brow and quickly let it fall as if to say, "We'll just see about that." No child was going to be left behind without the ability to read, write and do some simple math. She was a true educator at heart and intended to save this little girl from growing up illiterate. She conducted school as usual and at the end of the day, gave home work assignments. She then dismissed

class. Gathering up her belongings, out the door of
the school she went in a huff. Marching toward the
head of the hollow where Maysel and John lived, she
discovered that she was not as physically fit as she
thought she was. Walking uphill proved to be very
taxing on her, resulting in shortness of breath, but she
kept steady on until she was finally on the porch and
hearing the sounds of her very loud knocks on the
door. John was ever so slow to answer, but eventually
opened the door.

With a smart-assed tone of voice, he asked her,
"What do *you* want?"

"Did you get my note yesterday Mr. Brunty?"
she asked rather nicely.

"Yep. So?

"What do you mean, "So?"

"So?" he repeated.

Surely you intend to send your child to school
Mr. Brunty."

"Nope. Sure don't. She's not goin. No need for
Maysel to go to school. She belongs to me and I
don't want to send her, and I ain't goin to." He said
in ignorant, stubborn defiance.

"Really? Mrs. Hagerman said. "Well, here's the
rest of the story. Now listen and listen carefully Mr.
Brunty because this is a very important message for
you. It is also the *last* one before the authorities are
made aware of this matter. You may not be aware, but
it is *required* by law that all children of school age be
sent to school. It is *my* job to report these matters. I
am expecting Maysel to be enrolled in school no later
than tomorrow morning or I promise you that there

will be truant officers all over this place conducting a complete investigation of you. It's possible that you could face heavy monetary penalties if you do not comply. Maysel WILL attend school . . . one way or another. Am I making myself clear Mr. Brunty?

"Who in the hell do you think you are? You can't just come in and tell folks what they have to do and what they can't do!" He spit at her.

"Mr. Brunty. I don't *think* anything. I *know* my job and it is to see that every child in the area attends school. I refuse to stand here and argue with you about this any further. I have delivered this information. She must attend school and I'm sorry if that inconveniences you."

"I don't have money to buy pencils and paper for her." He lied. "She'll have to have books. I ain't got no money fur that neither." He announced as if that would make a difference in the law.

"With or without those items Mr. Brunty, she still MUST attend school and that's all I'm saying. Good day." And with a smile on her face, she departed and went home. Tomorrow would tell the tale.

Investigation? Officers? Fines? Holy cow! John couldn't have any of this at the cabin. Someone may discover "the business" and then what would he do? "Damn! I guess I'll just have to let her go to school," he thought. John hated defeat and resented this one nearly as much as when Lela refused to reconcile with him, but there was only one thing to do. He must send her. "Well, while she's at school, you can feed her too." He thought.

Mrs. Hagerman arrived a little early at school the

next day. She was eager to see if Maysel would show up. Other children began to arrive and she could hear them playing outside. They always did this until the bell rang. Albert Aliff proudly rang the bell 15 times as he did every morning. The students came in and took their designated seats and roll call began. Maysel was not present. At that time the door opened and stepping inside the doorway was a very shy and frightened little girl dressed in bib overalls and white tee shirt. With down-cast eyes, the child waited for her presence to be recognized by Mrs. Hagerman.

"Good morning." she said kindly. Observing this neglected sad child, Mrs. Hagerman immediately fell in love with her. She could not let herself do it, but she wanted to rush over to Maysel and put her arms around her and hug her. She thought Maysel was the most adorable thing she had ever seen. Her sandy blonde hair and those big, piercing blue eyes were enough to melt the heart of Satan. The fact that she was motherless accelerated a deep compassion in Mrs. Hagerman. The moment was very intense and one that this very caring and gifted teacher would never forget. The magnitude of the close relationship that would build in the near future was unknown to both Mrs. Hagerman and Maysel. "You must be John Brunty's little girl."

"Yes, Ma'am. My name is Maysel."

"Everyone please say 'Hello' to Maysel and make her feel welcome.

Almost in unison the class said, "Hello, Maysel."

There was an empty seat located almost beside

the teacher's desk and Mrs. Hagerman motioned for Maysel to be seated in it. Knowing that John had no intentions of furnishing Maysel with school supplies and books, Mr. Hagerman intended to share her own. Seating the child close to the teacher's desk would make that easier.

As she walked toward her seat near Mrs. Hagerman's desk, Maysel noticed that Wannie's seat was just behind hers. Before being seated, their eyes met and an impish, child-like smirk came over Wannie's face as if to say, "I won! You have to go to school too! Ha, Ha!" Maysel smiled and took her seat. Being forced to attend school was one of the most important incidents to occur in her young life, but Wannie did not know this. All he knew was that if he had to go to school, then every other kid in the hollow had to go too. This was a very lucky day for Maysel. School provided more than just an education for her. It also gave her the opportunity to form many friendships with other children, and a special bond with her teacher. So far, she had been isolated at the cabin and not allowed to socialize with other children in the hollow. The work details imposed on her by John were heavier than most adults could tolerate and left her with little time for anything else except sleep and rest. Wannie was the only student in the school that she really knew at this time, and she was very happy that he was kind to her. He would eventually prove to be her best friend.

Her first day of school turned out to be quite a joy. Most of the other girls had "best friends" and during lunch and recess, the students would pair up and separate into small groups. Maysel understood that it would take a while to be accepted into these "clubs" and busied herself during these times. Solitude was not a problem for her. She was used to it. John was not a good parent. Packing a lunch for Maysel was not on his list if important things to do. His attitude was that if Maysel had to go to school, not only could Mrs. Hagerman provide school supplies for her, but she could also feed her while she was at school, or she could just be hungry. That'll show her!

Some students lived close enough to walk home for lunch, but most of them carried their lunches in brown paper bags. They took their lunches outside to eat. In moments the food was gobbled down and they could continue playing. Maysel had no lunch, but she did have hunger. On this first day of school, she decided to stay inside alone so she would not be forced to watch the other children eating. Sitting in the back of the school room, she looked up and Wannie entered the room. Their eyes met, but not a word was spoken between the two innocent children. Wannie sat down in the seat across from Maysel and quietly removed a fried egg sandwich from it. "So much for avoiding seeing others eat." She thought. Then still not saying a word, Wannie tore his sandwich into two equal pieces and handed Maysel one. She hesitated, but her hunger won out. This gesture made her like Wannie even more. How kind. How considerate. "Hey, he really must like me to give me half his lunch!" she thought as she consumed his precious gift. This became a daily ritual for the following few years of school. Whatever was in Wannie's lunch, he gave Maysel half.

Maysel found school to be great! She loved Mrs. Hagerman and loved to learn. In no time, she knew all the other students by name and made friends with most. Although it was never mentioned, Maysel was the teacher's "pet." Life for Maysel was a battle ground and going to school proved to be no different. She only had to prove herself once by winning a fight with the school bully, Butch Accord who bullied everyone at school. Pick on Maysel . . . not wise. She kicked his rump royally and dared him to ever bully anyone else. She got her wish and also gained the respect of the entire school. No more trouble for her. Not after that victory. Since the conflict occurred after school and quite a distance from school, Maysel received no punishment. Mrs. Hagerman heard about the fight from other students, but she never mentioned it. I guess she considered that Maysel had just solved a long-term problem. For that, she was thankful. Hmmm . . . another reason to love Maysel.

Eagerness to learn and please her teacher motivated Maysel to excel in all of her studies. She could hardly wait to go to school. She had perfect attendance and maintained high grades. Mrs. Hagerman was very pleased with Maysel's progress. Attending school was not a bad thing and Maysel was convinced that this was going to be a very special treat. Learning was a delicious experience and she just could not get enough. School! Yummy!

Chapter 22

John was off on one of his "business" trips and had been gone for more than three days. Maysel was now eleven years old. Although no one but Mrs. Hagerman recognized it, she was blossoming into a young lady. John still was filled with resentment every time he looked at her. Maysel was the spitting image of her mother and was looking more like Lela every day. Unknown to Maysel, this was the reason for his being so unkind, unfair and even at times cruel to her. John felt that his bad treatment of Maysel would somehow punish Lela for rejecting him, punish her for not helping him save their relationship. He never once accepted full responsibility for all of the damage caused by his deception. The fact that Lela may have suffered irreparable emotional, spiritual and mental anguish never crossed his mind. He still wanted her to pay for her decision to terminate their "marriage." The seven wonderful, happy years that they shared together could not have happened had he revealed his marital status. Was she blind? Could she not see this? Well, Lela could just be spiteful and John could be even more so.

It was Saturday and Maysel sat on the porch
of their cabin enjoying the afternoon sun when she
looked down the hollow. Their front porch provided
a panoramic view. One could see at least one half
mile and detect any visitors long before their
arrival at the cabin. Three men on horseback were
coming up the winding road. It looked like the same
"Revenuers" that had visited two other times in the
past few weeks. Revenuers were Federal Agents who
look for moonshine stills. They usually tore down the
stills and prosecuted their owners. Maysel quietly
observed them for about ten minutes and decided that
she may need to prepare to go to the hole unless they
stopped to visit another resident. Nope. They just
kept coming. From past experience, she knew there
was plenty of time to "disappear" before their arrival
at the cabin. Her eyes scanned the cabin looking for
any signs of "shine." There were none. She looked
out the window and down the hollow once more to
assess the situation of the on-coming visitors. Yep.
They were getting nearer. She must make her move
right now.

Going out the back door and walking bent over,
she swiftly made her way to the "hole." Lifting the
"lid" just enough for passage, she went down the
ladder into the cool, dark space. She then let down
the "lid." Her eyes finally adjusted to the darkness of
the hole and she could vaguely see her surroundings.
Burlap coffee sacks lined the floor of the hole.
Resting on sizable stones, which kept moisture from
rotting them, wooden orange crates held many, many
corked bottles of "shine." Maysel had produced and

stored all of it alone. Storing the bottles in these boxes allowed her to stack them on top of each other, leaving more room for her to move around.

She seated herself in a comfortable position. Looking up, she could see through small separations between the saplings that formed the "lid." She waited and listened for on-coming voices. Hearing the rustling sounds of footsteps coming toward the hole, she made every effort to remain silent. The footsteps stopped just about two feet from the hole. Maysel was so tense. They were so close that she could actually see one of them through the small opening in the lid.

"I don't care what anybody says. John Brunty's got a still up here somewhere and I know it." One of them said.

"Well, we've been up here several times and we ain't found nothin' yet. We've looked this whole place over more than one time. If we don't find nothin,' then there's nothing we can do. It don't look like he's got one. We've looked everywhere for it. Cleave, what else can we do? We *know* he don't work and that he stays gone a lot on "business." A business that he says is *none* of *our* business. Our snitch says he "shines," so he's *got* to have a still somewhere. This man is really slick and if we can't *prove* it on him, then there's nothin' we can do, right?

"What you're sayin' is the truth Ralph, but how can we give up when our guts are tellin' us that we're right about this? Cleave said. The third man remained quiet.

Just then Ralph stepped very close to the hole. He

was so close that pieces of loose dirt fell from the top of the hole onto Maysel's face as she stared up at him through the small opening.

"Oh, my God! Please don't let him take another step closer. If he does, he's gonna fall in here right on top of me." She prayed.

Like an answer to Maysel's prayer, the men turned and went toward the back of the cabin. They took one more look around searching for the still that they were certain existed. They failed again. Maysel listened while they searched. In complete and total disbelief, the men finally left and as they did so, she heard one of them say, "We'll catch him. Sooner or later, we *will* catch him."

She listened as the men made their departure and when she felt it safe, she came out of the hole. She made her way to the back of the cabin and entered the back door. She ran to the window and glanced down the hollow. There they were. They were leaving the hollow. Thank God! That was a very close call. They had never been so close to the hole before. Maysel felt like she had dodged a bullet.

Evening came and darkness fell on the cabin. It was about 8:00 p.m. and Maysel heard John step upon the porch. When he entered, Maysel spoke to him, but he said nothing to her. He only nodded his head in her direction. She looked so much like Lela lately that John could hardly bear looking at her.

"Revenuers were here again today Poppy." She said.

"Oh yeah? Tell me about it." He said with a little interest.

"Well, ya know this is the third time in just a few weeks that they've come up here don't ya? Reminding him that things could be getting serious.

"I don't care if they camp out up here. They'll never find." He said. 'Besides, I've got me a job, a real job. They'll let up on me when I can prove that I have other work. It's called loggin'. There's coalmines that'll pay people for props. That's logs that are cut just the right length and ones that are just the right thickness. I could get good money for that. They use the props to hold the top of the mine up while the workers dig the coal out. Props keep the top of the mine tunnel from fallin' in on them. I already sealed the deal and we will start the middle of next week. Just you and me. We'll go into the woods, cut down the trees we need with a cross cut saw and pull them out of the woods with chains. Then we will measure them and cut them up to the right size." He even winked at her in an attempt to make this adventure sound like fun. Somehow, Maysel knew that this idea would turn out to be hard work.

Wednesday came and the new "job" would begin today. A new "mother-in-law" had showed up on Sunday. Her name was Nettie. She was a rather attractive brunette who dressed very feminine. Her hair was curled and stuffed into a large, heavy hairnet that was pulled back so that it hung down onto her shoulders in the back. The edge of the hairnet was anchored with hairpins across the crown of her head. Maysel was envious of her dresses and shoes. She even had perfume, lipstick and nail polish. Maysel had never seen any of these items before. There was something about this woman that made Maysel uncomfortable and for some reason Maysel didn't like her very well. Nettie was always giving John seductive looks that made him get a silly grin and a look on his face that Maysel did not understand. He seemed very fond of this woman and gave her a lot of very special attention. Maysel's bedroom had been the outdoors ever since Nettie's arrival. She hated sleeping outside. She knew what the sleeping arrangements were whenever "mother-in-laws" visited, but she still hated to leave her pallet on the floor to sleep outside. What an inconvenience.

John carried the saw and one large chain and Maysel carried the other large chain. Each of the chains was about twenty feet long and each had a huge hook on one end of it. Nettie carried nothing except her handbag . . . another item that Maysel had seen few of. As they walked toward the wooded area, Nettie complained that her wedged sandals would be ruined if she had to walk through all that brush. John put down his saw and chain, walked over to Nettie and picked her up in his arms and carried her to a clearing where he gently sat her on a big log that happened to be there. He then returned to Maysel and picked up the saw and chain and motioned Maysel to follow him. As they passed Nettie, now posing on the log as though she was being photographed, John gave her a kiss. In a tone of voice that was almost apologetic, he explained that they would be back shortly.

Into the woods the two of them went, leaving Nettie by herself. Looking around and choosing the perfect trees to be taken down, John positioned himself on one side of a tree and placed Maysel on the other side. Using the cross-cut saw, the two of them pulled the saw back and forth until the tree finally fell. They then removed the limbs from the tree, which reduced it to a long pole. As quickly as they could, they prepared another tree in the same manner. John demonstrated to Maysel how to wrap a chain around the end of the log and place the hook onto the longer end of the chain. Using the long end of the chain, they each pulled their log out of the woods by dragging it behind them.

Nettie heard them coming and was relieved that she was no longer alone. Poor thing was subjected to being bored and having to sit there while these two worked like brutes. She gave Maysel looks that seemed to say, "I'm better than you and I don't have to do any of this stuff, Ha, Ha." Nettie was only about seven years older than Maysel, which made thing even worse.

The logs were very heavy, but John and Maysel succeeded in delivering them to the clearing. There, they proceeded to cut them into the necessary lengths for sale to the coalmine. That finished, the two of them returned to the woods and continued for several hours cutting, dragging and creating "props" for the coal mine. There would be many more days like this in Maysel's life. Yep. Many more.

Maysel was miserable and the work was very taxing on her female frame, but she pushed herself to complete the tasks required of her. She did, however, get a little satisfaction from witnessing Nettie's discomfort. She could tell from the look on her face and by the way she squirmed that Nettie was just as miserable as she, maybe more. After all, Maysel was conditioned to hard work, but it was clear that Nettie was not accustomed to being in any uncomfortable situations. Maysel turned her back towards Nettie and a gentle smile of contentment came on her face. "Just wait until about dark Nettie." Maysel thought. "You have been a smart-aleck and have made fun of me this blessed day. Suffer is what you're gonna do tonight and tomorrow. You fool, sitting there posing like a fashion model all day, in a low-cut sundress. Pull that dress tail up a little farther for Poppy. Go ahead, this is getting better. *I've* been shaded by being in the woods most of the day, but you? You're so silly that you're not even aware that YOU HAVE BEEN IN THE SUN ALL DAY!" Maysel could hardly wait for evening to come.

As they returned to the cabin, John carried Nettie to a place where she could walk without ruining her precious shoes and then returned to carry the saw and his chain. Maysel followed behind and wanted to laugh out loud, but didn't. This fun would be hers and hers alone. She noticed the bright, hot pink sunburn on the front and back of Nettie's neck and shoulders. Her arms looked as if they could glow in the dark, and her legs would be on fire this evening. Let the fun begin.

A pot of beans had been left cooking on the stove all day. They smelled good and would be ready to eat in time for supper. Maysel peeled and fried some potatoes, remembering to save the skins for their hogs at Mr. Varney's. Her mind was not on cooking right now. There was very little entertainment in her life, but she was certain that she would enjoy tonight's show. Nettie's display today would be topped by tonight's performance. And Maysel was getting anxious. "Let the show begin!" She thought.

During their evening meal, there was very little conversation. John spoke of the money that he would collect from sale of the props and made several statements concerning that. He never thanked Maysel for her efforts today. Neither did he offer to share the money with her. He just considered Maysel an extension of himself–not an individual. She was just another beast of burden to him.

Dark had come and by now Nettie had begun to notice the burning sensations on the various parts of her body. She began to complain about the discomfort associated with the sunburn that was making its presence known. Maysel noticed that the bright pink color of this afternoon had changed to a deep, hot, fiery red. This should be good.

Bedtime arrived and the three of them prepared to sleep. John and Nettie would sleep in the bed and Maysel would sleep outside. Maysel really hated leaving Nettie because she wanted to enjoy her suffering, but she was instructed to leave. Fluffing her mattress made of leaves and hay, she could hear the sounds of suffering coming from the cabin. Yes, poor Nettie was paying for the fun of basking in the sun and posing seductively for Poppy all day. Lying outside in the dark, Maysel could hear Nettie moaning and groaning. Hmm. These moans and groans had a different tone to them than the ones Maysel had heard coming from the cabin during the past three nights.

Maysel rested and waited for sleep to come while she listened to the sounds of Nettie's agony. She did enjoy it and sleep did come.

Rising the next morning and entering the cabin, Maysel discovered that neither John nor Nettie had slept much that night. John had spent most of the night dipping rags in cool water and applying them to Nettie's burns. This was a good thing, because Maysel would not have to "log" today. John was too tired and Nettie's sunburn was giving a new meaning to "hot tamale'"

Chapter 23

Lela and Jack had met two years ago. Theirs had been a long "engagement." Jack determined that he *would* marry Lela, even if the wait was *ten* years. He had been blessed with an abundance of patience. Always even-tempered and calm, he had a lifetime to wait for Lela. His interest in other women had ended. The longer he knew Lela the more he wanted to marry her . . . at any cost. Making the decision to marry had been a difficult (if not an impossible) task for Lela. She still felt the sting from her previous "marriage" to Frank Adams. The nightmare that he had put her through was still fresh in her mind and losing her only child through his heinous act was extremely painful to live with. A lot had transpired during the past two years, but one thing that had not changed was Lela's dedication to her parents. It was more than apparent to Jack that Lela would *never* move to the Charleston area. If he was to pursue a romance with her it would have to be in Greenbrier County. After meeting the Pittsenbargers, Jack quickly sensed the very tight bond of this family . . . a bond that not even the strongest romance could break. Yep. He had to leave Charleston and find employment near her . . . so he did.

Jack began working in a coal mine near the Pittsenbargers. He soon made progress in his pursuit of Lela. He had moved into a small house not far from her and was trying desperately to prove his willingness to sacrifice, provide a home and make a good living for her. His kind nature had given him an obsession for helping Lela in her search for Maysel. This alone meant more to Lela than anyone knew. Jack had every quality women look for in a man, but he only had eyes for Lela and he had finally convinced her to marry him. Their love was rare and genuine and it was one that would endure until they both were dead.

Still problematic was the "divorced woman" stigma that plagued Lela's wedding plans. She had let loose and allowed herself to fall in love with Jack Trout and she wanted the world to know it, but making a big to-do of her *second* wedding could not happen. She had discussed her situation with the church minister and he explained that under the circumstances; her "marriage" was neither legal nor binding. In fact, Lela had never "really" been married at all and her marriage to *Jack* would be recognized as her first. Even so, she decided her wedding would be a small one with only Mama, Papa, Lela and Jack attending. Big, small, inside, outside, church, J. P., minister, attendants, it made no difference to Jack. He was concerned only that the wedding *was* taking place anywhere, anytime, anyplace. Jack was a wise and patient man. Lela's history made him aware of her mental, emotional, spiritual and social damage. He had committed himself to helping her find Maysel. Jack was convinced that their love could dissolve all bad memories from her past and help fade them from her mind forever.

Looking picturesque, the small wedding party emerged from the office of the Justice of the Peace. Lela wore a sky blue suit (nothing white!) with a matching hat that saddled her head and covered the upper portion of her face with a veil of netting. Carrying a small bouquet of fresh flowers and a testament, she looked radiant. Mama's dress was of a soft floral fabric with a hem line that flared slightly. She also sported a hat that resembled Lela's. Jack and Poppy wore their Sunday best. They headed to the church. Lela's friends had insisted on giving the reception as a wedding gift from them all. The church was filled with congratulations from well-wishers. Love filled the room as well as the hearts of everyone in attendance. The efforts of all their friends pleased Lela and Jack very much. A beautiful and tasteful affair, it was also a memorable one. Expensive professional photographers were not affordable, but Lela and Jack had their own memories of the day to help them relive their wedding day.

No one except the wealthy was financially able to go on a honeymoon. Jack and Lela, being no different, went directly home to begin their new life together. Their honeymoon would last a lifetime.

Chapter 24

Mrs. Hagerman and Maysel had formed a very special bond. Theirs was a true, fun relationship that the teacher shared with no other student. Maysel believed that although she was the poorest child in the school, she was also the most fortunate for having this special friendship with Mrs. Hagerman. She strived to excel in her studies so that Mrs. Hagerman would be proud of her. She kept her teacher on a very high pedestal and Maysel absolutely adored and respected her beyond words. Having "teacher time" was now the most important thing in Maysel's life. Almost every Sunday, Maysel was allowed to spend the day with Mrs. Hagerman. John benefited from this arrangement too. Maysel was supervised and he was free to spend his time with women. Hey, this set-up wasn't too bad. Everyone wins! Right?

Yep! Sundays were the highlight of her week. She literally lived for these days when she could just do girly things with her beloved friend and teacher. The hard labors of the week seemed easier if she concentrated on Sundays.

The changes in Maysel's body were becoming

noticeable. She would mature soon and it appeared that she would be very well endowed. Sharing Maysel's dislike for bib overalls, Mrs. Hagerman selected three dresses of her own to share with Maysel. The dresses were altered to better fit Maysel's blooming figure and she was allowed to wear them during Sunday visits. They feared John would destroy them had he known about them. How proudly she would strut and parade in these fashions. The two would giggle, laugh and pretend to be rich folk by having lemonade and indulging in chitchat with each other. Whenever there was a minister in the area, the teacher would even allow Maysel to wear these dresses with some of her shoes to church. Maysel hated the "uniform" of bibbed overalls and tee shirt, which John demanded her to wear. Like any other twelve-year-old girl, Maysel wanted to wear dresses. She desired to be feminine and to be clean, look nice and just be a normal adolescent female. The only perfume available to her was a little vanilla flavoring or to wipe the fragrance of roses and honeysuckle onto her skin. Whenever she did this, Poppy made all manners of fun of her. It never dawned on him that Maysel was becoming a young lady and he certainly could not fathom that she was a real person with feelings, emotions and basic needs. Being a "real" person would cloud the reality that he needed her to make his living. Besides, she was dumb and knew no better. People are creatures of habit and Maysel's habit was to work very hard for him. Yep, she sure made a good living for him. After all, he was one of the first people in West Virginia to own an automobile and he never worked at public works. How questionable is that?

Being absent from school for two days was a very unusual occurrence for Maysel. Aware of Maysel's passion for school, Mrs. Hagerman suspected her to be either sick, or that John had taken her from the hollow for some reason. At any rate, she would get to the bottom of this mystery. It was unlike Maysel to be tardy, let alone be absent. Her history showed that she was in school if no one else was. Indeed, something was very wrong here!

"Wannie, would you do me a favor?"

"Yes, Mrs. Hagerman."

"I'd like you to deliver this note to Maysel after school today. Now, Wannie, it is VERY important that she get this note immediately after school. You won't delay, now will you?"

"No, Ma'am. I'll take it straight to her. I promise." Wannie said with a tone of seriousness in his voice that made the teacher believe him.

Maysel was at home alone and facing what she thought to be certain death. Yesterday and today had been a horrible experience for her. Her mind flashed back over the past few years as she recalled vivid memories of death occurring from great losses of blood. Slaughtering hogs, chickens and other small animals was commonplace for her. The throat of a hog was cut from ear to ear and it was allowed to bleed to death before the meat was dressed out for use at the table. By association, she was convinced that her time to die had arrived. She had tried everything she knew to stop the profuse bleeding which had started yesterday morning, but nothing worked. Poppy had showed her to apply cold water from the spring to any bleeding wound and that would help stop the bleeding. It worked on her hand the day Poppy had accidentally cut it on a cross-cut saw, but not this time. Nope. Not working. To make matters worse, there were no rags with which to apply cold water.

"Wait," she had thought yesterday as she was bleeding. "I do have some fabric."

In a panic, her eyes shifted to the pallet on which she slept each night. Grasping the corner of the pallet and giving it one quick jerk revealed her most prized possession. It was the tiny dress that she was wearing seven years earlier when John brought her to the hollow at age five. It was also the one she had worn in the photo taken of her on her fifth birthday. She never got to see the photo. This little dress was the source of many memories for Maysel. She remembered her mother dressing her lovingly in it for the "fair" and she remembered dancing around the room with it for fun during times when John left her alone for long periods of time. She lifted the wrinkled, treasured garment and looked at it. Having no choice, she ripped it into long pieces. She had rushed outside to the spring and dipped out a bucket of cold water, drenched the rags in it and applied them to her bleeding self. She held the cold wet rags on the bleeding area for as long as she could tolerate it, but nothing seemed to help stop the bleeding. Maysel had lain down with a cold wet rag on her genitals to wait for either death to occur or for the bleeding to stop by some miracle. She was very frightened.

Hearing a knock on the door was the very last thing that Maysel needed to hear. Bang, bang, bang Wannie's hand rapped on the door so loud that it startled her.

"Maysel! Maysel!" He yelled. "Open the door. I have a note from the teacher for ya."

"Go away, Wannie. Leave me alone." She yelled back at him through the closed door.

"Mrs. Hagerman said it was very important that I give you this note and I have to give it to ya. Open up!" He pleaded.

Being very careful not to be seen by him, Maysel opened the door just enough to retrieve the note from his hand. "Thanks." She said, "Now, please go home." She slammed the door shut.

"Are you comin to school tomorrow?

"Maybe, *go home!*" She said firmly through the closed door.

She hurriedly opened the note and read it. Mrs. Hagerman simply ordered her to come to her house immediately. She had emphasized the word NOW.

"Oh, my God! I can't go to her house like this! I'm dying!" She thought.

Yet she respected Mrs. Hagerman and did her very best to conceal her problem. Although there was a huge dark spot on the seat of her bib overalls, she put them on. This was the only clothing that she had. Wearing the soiled overalls, she left home quickly and arrived at the teacher's house in a matter of minutes.

Maysel knocked lightly on the door, but refused the invitation to enter the house. Remaining on the porch, she was joined by Mrs. Hagerman. After making eye contact with Maysel, Mrs. Hagerman became alarmed. Maysel's eyes were so red and swollen that they looked painful. She looked at Mrs. Hagerman through tiny slits and a streak of fear shot through the older woman. Dreading the unthinkable (that her father had possibly molested her) she moved close to Maysel and in a very compassionate voice said, "Maysel, what's wrong?

Avoiding eye contact with her teacher and friend, on the porch and staring down at the floor. "Nothin." She said. Telling a lie to this wonderful woman was most difficult.

Evermore thinking the worst now, Mrs. Hagerman pulled Maysel's face around so she could see it and said, "Maysel, look at me. Tell me what's wrong. Now, something's very wrong here, and you need to tell me what it is. It doesn't matter how *bad* it is, you can tell *me*. You can tell me *anything*, Darlin' . . . anything at all. Now, will you please tell my why you have been crying so hard?"

Maysel finally looked at her and said, "I'm dying, Mrs. Hagerman. I know I am. I just know it."

"Die? What on earth makes you think that?

"I'm gonna bleed to death." Maysel said as her memory revisited the bleeding, dying animals in the hog pen.

"Where are you bleeding from, Maysel?

"Down there." Maysel said as she pointed to her genital area.

With a look of surprise on her face, Mrs. Hagerman said, "Oh, that. Aunt Flow"

"Aunt who? Maysel was really confused now. At this time, she certainly didn't want to be visited by relatives or anyone else for that matter. She was in no condition for company.

"Now, you just come on in the house with me. We need to talk. And, by the way, you're not gonna die. You're gonna be just fine." Laughing and taking Maysel by the hand, she led her into the house.

Mrs. Hagerman was a very together type of a woman. Smart, organized, clean and always efficient, she had an aura of enthusiasm that seemed to surround her. God had blessed her with a lot of patience, joy, optimism and love, which often seemed to fill entire rooms when she entered them. Maysel was totally convinced that the teacher had all the answers to everything.

Instructing Maysel not to sit on her furniture, but to stand in the center of the room, she left the room. Readily, she returned with a flour sack full of rags and dumped them onto the middle of the floor beside Maysel. She left the room again and returned with a pan of warm water, some soap and a towel. The next words from her mouth were a great relief to Maysel.

"Maysel, Every woman has this problem. After reaching a certain age, all women have spells when they bleed like this. It happens every month and lasts about a week. You'll experience it about every twenty-eight days.

"This happens to you too? Maysel asked.

"Every month, just as you will from now on. Every month, every month, every month, until you are about fifty years old or so. Make no mistake about it. It will always happen. Now Maysel, you must stay prepared for this each and every month. You don't want to be in school or somewhere and have a huge spot of blood appear on the seat of your pants. Do you? She asked.

Maysel wondered why Mrs. Hagerman wasn't too concerned about all the blood she had lost these past two days. "Why does this happen? Maysel asked.

"It just does. We all have to put up with it. It's called the "plague." Just something women have had to put up with since the beginning of time. Now, let's get you cleaned up and I'll show you how to make the "bandages" for yourself."

Mrs. Hagerman selected a couple of nice sized rags and fashioned a feminine napkin from them and laid them aside. With some reluctance, Maysel undressed at the bidding of the older woman. In the presence of anyone else, she would have fought like a panther to remain clothed. Maysel was very modest, but this lady had a calming effect on her. She trusted Mrs. Hagerman completely and listened while her friend taught her how to clean herself, how to use the bandages and how to prevent odors. Maysel was given two flour sacks. One contained rags and the other was empty. The soiled "bandages" were to be placed in the empty one. When "Aunt Flow's" visit was over, Maysel was to bring both bags to Mrs. Hagerman's house for washing and recycling. The two women must boil them in a tub full of water and lye soap, dry them and place them back into the flour sack to await the next "visit."

"I don't have any rags at my house. I tore up

my little dress yesterday and used it try and stop the bleeding. That's all the rags I have."

"I have plenty here. I've been plagued with this for a long time." She said with a chuckle in her voice, which seemed to comfort Maysel. The teacher's smile assured the younger woman that this was "no big deal" and nothing to worry about.

As Maysel left Mrs. Hagerman's house and headed back up the hollow, she was very relieved that she wasn't going to die. She truly thought she was a goner there for a while. It seemed impossible that any living creature could lose that quantity of blood and still survive. Even with the bad news that this would occur every month, Maysel was thankful that she was going to live, and from her heart, this innocent child thanked God for allowing her to live longer.

With a thankful heart and hoping to avoid any encounters with neighbors on her way home, she hurried up the hollow. Poppy could return any at any time and her overalls were in bad need of laundering. He could not know about her visit from "Aunt Flow." That matter was far too personal to be discussed with anyone, let alone Poppy!

Chapter 25

Married for two years now, Jack and Lela were living a very happy life. With the exception of growing stronger, his love for her never changed. He adored her and was proud that his entire life revolved around her. Likewise, she loved and admired Jack. Theirs was truly a happy marriage. Only one thing was lacking . . . children. Conception was not happening for them in spite of their many attempts. It looked as though God's plan for their lives did not include children. They finally accepted being childless and never complained about that subject again.

Maysel would be ten years old by now, but Lela had never ceased searching for her. Without modern communication technology such as television, Internet, telephones etc., it was practically impossible to locate a missing child in 1933. The only source of information at Lela's disposal was word of mouth. Jack and Lela's eyes and ears were always fine-tuned to any clue that might lead them to the missing child.

Jack worked very hard providing for Lela. Their needs were met, but they lived frugally. He pinched every penny and made daily contributions of money to a cookie jar. This was money set aside to finance Lela's *many* searches for Maysel. Jack stayed home while Lela searched. He was compassionate about her loss and was of great comfort to her. For that, Lela was grateful.

The unusual name, *Maysel*, led Lela in many directions in search of her. People were cruel to give her false clues, but she had to investigate each one. So far, all leads were dead ends and there was no Maysel at the end of her searches. Sure, Lela was disappointed many, many, times after her searches ended with nothing, but her faith in God's promise to her stayed ever strong. She loved the song, 'Standing on the Promises of God" and sang it almost daily, which seemed to enrich her faith. Her Papa had taught her never to be without a song. "There's not enough devils in Hell to make me doubt what God promised me about seeing Maysel again," She often said, "*He* told me that I'll see her again. *He* said it, *I* believe it and it's so." Deep depression would never be her companion again. God had raised her up and God would be her strength, just as He had promised.

The searches were exhausting and when she returned from each one, Lela would just collapse into bed for a day or two. Jack was very patient and considerate at these times. He knew how physically and emotionally drained she was every time she ventured out, so he made her as comfortable as possible and waited for her to regain her energy.

The large, framed photo of five-year-old Maysel sat on Lela's dresser. She stared at it often as numerous thoughts flooded her mind. How desperately she wanted to hold her little girl. There were so many unanswered questions about her disappearance that may never be answered. How long would it be before she saw her again? Why did Frank do such an evil thing? Will Maysel remember her mother? Is Maysel alright? Is she fed? Is she warm? Is she cold? Is he teaching her the ways of God? The list of questions was endless. The photo was the only piece of identification for the missing child and it accompanied Lela on all her searches. She hoped and prayed that someone would recognize Maysel by looking at it. Maysel's appearance had surely changed in the past five years and the likelihood that anyone would recognize her from the photo was becoming less and less. Lela carried it with her anyway, because it was all she had left of her daughter and it seemed to give her a sense of connection.

In addition to everything else that Lela had to deal with, she also had to fight another demon . . . hate. A lot of prayer was required to maintain a clean heart. She had to pray for spiritual cleansing daily because it is human nature to hate anyone who wrongs your child. Hating Frank would be so easy. At times she wished him dead. She wished horrible, painful, long-term illnesses on him. In some of her emotional moments, she felt that she had the ability to kill him with her bare hands. In her mind, she could feel her fingers tearing through his flesh and ripping at it until life was gone from his body. These thoughts and feelings were not Godly and Lela had to continually pray for God's love and peace to comfort her and protect her from them. It was a daily battle, but she would pray . . . and peace would come.

Just when you think you have God figured out, He proves you wrong. After three years of marriage and having no children God blessed this wonderful, loving couple with a child. No, not their own, but God made it possible for them to adopt a nine-week old baby boy whose mother had died. Her five children had to be placed in different homes. Edwin was the pride and joy of their lives. Filling their home with love and happiness, he became the center of their attention. He never replaced Maysel in Lela's heart, but he did an excellent job at filling his own place in the hearts and lives of Lela and Jack. They loved him as if he was theirs biologically. Their need to have a child was met and a child's need for a family was met. How fortunate this family was to be united by God's hand. Perfect.

Chapter 26

At thirteen, Maysel found herself still living in Laurel Branch Hollow. She was attending school and was in the seventh grade. She still maintained a good relationship with Mrs. Hagerman and, although her visits were less frequent, she still loved the teacher. More and more of her spare time over the past two years had been spent mostly with Wannie McCarty. John was not aware of this, because he spent so much time away on "business" to notice. He just assumed Maysel to be alright even if she was left without adult supervision for long periods of time.

Maysel had the body of a 15-year-old and the physical attraction between her and Wannie was growing in leaps and bounds. What starts out in *fun* usually ends up in *trouble*. Nature was taking its course and the two had begun having behavior of an adult nature for the past few months. In the experimental stage, they had a lot of exploring to do. At sixteen Wannie had desires that were becoming very difficult for him to contain and ones that he knew very little about. His very presence could bring out feelings in Maysel that she also knew nothing about.

In their innocence, they only knew that when alone together, they both become flushed, their hearts beat very fast and their breathing became short and faster. They wanted to touch each other and when they did, these feelings were accelerated. Their skin seemed to burn in an exciting, passionate and strange way. Wannie's gentle touch immediately brought goose bumps along her arms that exploded in thrills all over her body. Whatever was *wrong* with them when this happened, they liked it. It made them feel so good that eventually, their shyness was pushed aside and they enjoyed some very heavy petting. They feared the unknown, but there was an invisible power over them that forced them to satisfy their curiosity and desires. They "played it by ear" so to speak. If Wannie wanted to do it, then Maysel did too. He kissed, fondled, explored, petted, and caressed her until they both wanted to scream. She trusted him completely. No one had ever been as good to her as he was. They really loved each other, but neither of them knew a thing about love . . . and even less about making love.

This particular evening, John left on "business." As he left the cabin, he announced that he would be back in a couple of days. In addition to her regular responsibilities, he left Maysel with a number of other details. This, I am sure, was intended to keep her occupied and to prevent idle time. He left and she found herself alone, but not for long.

As soon as Wannie saw John pass on his way out of the hollow, he made a beeline to Maysel. Immediately on his arrival, the "magic power" came over them. They looked like beautiful paintings to each other in the soft light from the oil lamp on the table. It provided just enough light for them to see clearly the things they didn't understand. It also cast their shadows in soft dark silhouettes on the wall. The chirping of crickets coming from outside sounded like music to them. In no time, Maysel was standing there in front of him. This was as close to an affirmation as she could offer at only thirteen. Passion was so high that neither could speak. Gazing into each other's eyes in silence was the limit of their communication.

He toyed with a button on the chest of her overalls and slowly moved his hand to the side allowing his shaking fingers to slip between her bibs and her tee shirt. The thin cotton shirt was the only barrier between the back of his fingers and her two well-developed mounds. Maysel just stood there looking at him, and made no effort to reject his advances. She thought he was the most handsome guy around. Looking at him made her head turn around-n-round-n-round. Her trust in him could not be surpassed and yet, somehow, she occasionally made him unhappy with some of her unforgivable behavior. But this would not happen today. Today would be special. She would have no part in offending him today, no matter what his wishes were. He was the only person who seemed to care about her or showed her any consideration. Short of him, Maysel's life was completely void of affection.

Moments later, the straps on her bib overall had

been unhooked and the top peeled down to her waist. Wannie was kissing her and fondling her breasts. His hands were now under the tee shirt and he gently played with her erect nipples. Surprised that Maysel did not stop him, he continued. Cautiously, he lifted the tee shirt and gazed at her perky, swollen, young breasts as he lowered his lips to them. The wet contact of his mouth took Maysel's breath away and made her chest rise and fall as she inhaled and exhaled. Even if she wanted to stop him, her power of resistance was zero.

His head was on her chest and his mouth moved all over her breasts. Maysel buried her fingers in his thick, brown hair. The smell of him made her weak with desire and she loved it.

Together, their bodies sank to the floor of the shabby cabin. They continued stroking, caressing, kissing, fondling and breathing heavily for the next ten or fifteen minutes. Overcome by passion and desire, they had practically undressed each other. The hard wooden floor made them uncomfortable, so the couple moved to Maysel's pallet on the floor near by. It was there in the capacity of a childhood friendship that a true and long-term love first started to grow. The inevitable happened. Maysel knew in her heart that she would love him each and every day to the end of time.

Life offers an ultimate pleasure and they had experienced it, but they had loved each other long before this occurred. Young love had blossomed and there was nothing like it.

Chapter 27

Opening her eyes and dreading to face the morning, Maysel turned over from her night's sleep on her pallet. She had been awakened by an intense ray of sunlight beaming through the window. Its heat had been caressing her face and shoulder for the past ten minutes and she felt as though she was being hugged by Mother Nature. It felt warm, bright, comforting and soothing which made her think of Wannie. She loved him so much and to please him was high on her list of important things. He was the first thing on her mind every morning and the last thing on her mind when sleep would overcome her at night. He showed up frequently. He visited every day and came twice if he could finish his chores soon enough. In their innocent, naïve, unlearned state of being, neither was aware of the serious consequences their frolicking would produce. They knew nothing about "the birds and the bees." Taboo? Bad luck? Whatever the reason, adults did not discuss such things with their youth and as a result, teenage pregnancies were common.

Uh oh . . . now it was time for reality. The sick

feeling of nausea was creeping up inside her as it had done every morning for the past few weeks. As soon as she awoke, she knew she would be sick. Like all the other times, she scrambled to her feet, put her hand over her mouth and bolted out the door to puke.

"I don't know what this is." She thought, "I'm never sick and I've been throwing up every blessed morning. Maybe I'll get better soon and it'll stop." Thinking it was something she was eating that disagreed with her stomach, Maysel was oblivious to "morning sickness." At any rate, this was the last morning for her to tolerate it. The sickness would subside.

Catching her breath and walking back into the cabin, the feel of fabric brushed across her legs, which made her feel a little more feminine. The long cotton nightshirt that Mrs. Hagerman had given her was the only resemblance of a dress that she owned. Maysel loved it. She had discovered it to be very comfortable and so she slept in it. What an improvement to sleeping in her overalls. Well, she couldn't sleep *naked*, could she?

Glancing down over the front of her body, Maysel noticed that she seemed to be getting fat. It made her think of Mr. Clay, a man who lived down the hollow. Resembling a Buddha, his stomach was huge, round and hung way over his belt.

Maysel rubbed her hand gently over her belly and thought, "The last thing I want to do is get fat like Mr. Clay. If I don't eat much, then maybe I won't look like him."

She peeled out of the nightshirt and stepped into

her overalls that had become very snug. Maysel struggled to fasten the snaps and buttons, which was now required more effort to achieve. The task finally accomplished, she began her usual day of labor. John had been gone for almost two days and she expected him any time. "Shine" needed to be run, bottled and corked, a new vat of mash needed to be started. The chickens needed feeding, eggs needed to be collected, the horse needed feed and water, the cow needed to be milked and if she hurried, she could hoe some in the garden before the sun became too hot that day. She would check the garden for ripe vegetables and if there were any, she would gather them. Hopefully, there would be enough to last for two or three days. She may even stash some to share with Wannie. He also had labored in the garden and most certainly deserved its rewards.

Nearly five months had passed since the consummation of Wannie and Maysel's love for each other and these affections were now a part of their daily life. It was wonderful, fulfilling and satisfying. Neither of them saw harm in these activities. The word pregnant was absent from their vocabularies. Neither of them knew how babies were made. They were just doing what comes naturally. She looked forward to his visits, but if Poppy was at home, Wannie didn't come.

In the distance she heard the sound of an automobile. Rushing to the window she looked out and saw a very nice-looking Model A Ford making its way up the hollow.

"Oh, God, wonder who *that* is? Rich revenuers? It looks like they're driving cars now. I've got way too many things to do for them to be comin up here, and if I don't get most of it done, Poppy will kill me!" She thought, as she mentally prepared to "disappear." She decided to observe the approaching vehicle and wait until the driver was identified. No need to panic just yet. There was still time to make the dash for cover.

With a "bird's eye view" Maysel watched as the vehicle came to a halt and parked between the cabin and the bottom of the hill. The driver stepped out of the vehicle and she was surprised to see that it was Poppy. Wow! She almost didn't recognize him. He had bought himself an automobile, and was sporting some new clothes. Dressed in brown dress pants, a white shirt with suspenders and some new shiny shoes, he looked very much like an important businessman. Well, so much for Wannie's visit today.

Running from the cabin down to where the car was parked, Maysel couldn't believe her eyes. Poppy has a car! Before Poppy could get away from the car, Maysel was sitting in the passenger's seat touching and fingering the dash and touching the steering wheel, rolling the window up and down and peering over her shoulder to look out the back window. John was so proud that he couldn't wait to demonstrate how the trunk would transform into a seat.

"This is called a rumble seat. Some folks call it a "Mother-in-law's" seat, but your mothers-in-law will never ride back there." He said with a loud laugh, and started walking toward the cabin and motioned

Maysel to follow.

"Poppy. Take me for a ride in it. Please take me. I ain't never rode in a car before."

"I will, but first I have to go to the cabin." He said, never missing a step.

His promise to someday own a car had been fulfilled. The labor of a stolen child was the means by which he had made these purchases, but did John have any guilt? No, and he never would have any. Did it matter to him that Maysel had pulled logs from the woods with a chain and cut them up for props and that she had produced all the "shine" for him to sell? No, and it never would. How could he wear new clothes and look at his only daughter dressed so shabbily? How could he?

The two walked toward the cabin with Maysel in the lead. With a look of awe and disbelief on his face, John looked back several times as if the vehicle would not be there when he glanced again. If he didn't have a line-up of women, he would now. He had a vehicle, a lady magnet.

As they walked, John couldn't help noticing how much weight Maysel seemed to be gaining. Her overalls were snug and her belly was larger than usual.

"Am I gonna have to buy you another pair of overalls? Seems like that pair's gittin' too little for you." John remarked.

"I *am* gittin' fat. I hope my belly don't end up lookin like Mr. Clay's." Maysel innocently said.

"Hey. He's got one big gut. I hope you don't end up lookin like him either."

202 My Name is Maysel

They went inside and John made the announcement that he would be picking Nettie up to bring her to the cabin for the weekend. Maysel could come along and that would be her ride in the car.

Maysel and John were soon in the car. John pushed the starter and grinned at the sound of the motor. He put it into gear and down the hollow they went. Maysel was overwhelmed and proud as the neighbors watched them going buy. John was the only person in the entire hollow to be driving a car. Even though he was a lazy, self-centered bastard and treated Maysel so unfairly, he was still her father and she was proud that he had accomplished buying a car and some new clothes. It never entered her mind to be envious. Children can often forgive their parents for the most abusive treatment.

When Nettie saw them drive up in the car she threw both hands over her chest as if having a heart attack. Her eyes were wide open and the surprise on her face was priceless to John. He beamed with pride and strutted proudly as he opened the rumble seat for Maysel and held the door open for Nettie to be seated in the passenger's seat. With everyone in their places, they rode off in the direction of the cabin. Maysel was having such a good time, until it was ruined by the fact that she would have to sleep outside tonight. She had a "Mother-in-law" for a night, maybe two.

It was late afternoon and the three of them had finished having dinner and Maysel was cleaning up the dishes. In an attempt to ridicule Maysel, John made mention of Maysel's weight gain and compared it to looking like Mr. Clay. Nettie didn't laugh nor did she poke fun at Maysel. She got a serious look on her face and said, "This is *not* funny."

"What's not funny? John asked. "What's the matter with you?

Nettie pulled John close so she could whisper in his ear. John looked at Maysel's belly and his mouth dropped open a little. He heaved a sigh and said, "Do you really think so? As he stared at the swollen belly, the reality hit him.

"Looks like it to me." Nettie said with confidence.

"You could be right. Yeah, looks like it to me too, now that you mention it." He said in disappointment.

"What? Maysel asked. "What are y'all talkin' about?"

"Maysel, we don't think you're gittin fat, we think you might be knocked up." John said as if this term meant something anything to Maysel.

"I don't know what that is." Maysel said.

"You don't know what 'knocked up' is? Nettie asked as if she couldn't believe her ears.

"No, I don't. What is it? Maysel wanted to know.

"Dummy. We think you're gonna have a baby." Poppy said in a disgusted tone of voice.

"God's gonna give me a baby? Where's it coming from? I don't need a baby, but if He wants to give me one, I guess I'll take it." Maysel said with the innocence of a seven-year-old.

"Well, if we're right," Poppy said, "it's growing inside your belly right now and you ain't really just gittin fat. It's a dern youngin." He said as he waved his arms and held his hands around in the direction of Maysel's belly.

"Damn, I hope it ain't so. That's just what I need . . . another mouth to feed." With his elbows on the table and his head in his hands, he stared down at the table. Nettie placed her hand on his shoulder to comfort him.

Without looking up, John asked, "Who's is it?

"I guess it's mine." Maysel answered.

"No, I mean, who's the father?

"You just told me God was givin' me a baby." She said.

"You're just too dumb to talk to. I just hope it ain't so." He said shaking his head and muttering under his breath, "I'll kill him, I'll absolutely kill him."

John stood up and left the cabin to catch his breath and calm down. Nettie asked Maysel to join her at the table so she could question her about her condition.

"Maysel do you get visits from "Aunt Flow?

"I used to, but I ain't had one for about five times now. I don't miss it at all. I hope I never have another one. That would suit me just fine."

Swollen belly, no visit from Aunt Flow, this pregnancy was confirmed and Nettie calculated Maysel to be about five months. She had never displayed any compassionate feeling for Maysel in the past, but when John came back inside and began badgering Maysel, Nettie came to her defense and distracted John from the issue of discussion.

"John honey," she cooed, "leave her alone. If it *is* true, and she *is* knocked up, raisin cane ain't gonna change it, and besides, we've had such a good time today what with you buyin' a car, sportin' new clothes, lookin so fine and all. Please now, let's enjoy the rest of the evening." She said seductively as she pouted her mouth and ran her finger across his chest.

This issue had interrupted John's comfort zone and he was relieved when he didn't have to discuss it further. He never asked Maysel another question about it. He had not explained to Maysel about periods and conception and he most certainly would not be the one to explain what she could expect during the delivery of her baby. His attitude was that she had gotten herself into this mess and she'd have to get herself out of it, without him.

Later that week when Wannie could visit Maysel, she told him that God was giving her a baby. Wannie was a little excited. He loved babies, but would not realize until later what a major role he had played in its production. They just waited to see what would happen. He knew less than Maysel about procreation.

John avoided home as much as possible during the next four months. He came home only when necessary to check on things or maybe pick to up some "shine" that he had sold. Maysel saw very little of him and was relieved that his interrogation was short, but she didn't like it when John would call her Mr. Clay.

Maysel received no help to prepare her for the event of childbirth. They just left her uninformed and assumed that she would figure it out on her own. She was curious as to what magic trick her body would use to let the baby out. She felt certain that it had something to do with her belly button. That's it. The baby would somehow come from her belly button.

Chapter 28

Ever so constant in his effort to avoid Maysel, John had little to say to her during the remainder of her pregnancy. His great disappointment in her was a huge mystery. What did he expect? He was the adult here. He was the parent and was the responsible party in the matter. He was the negligent one, not Maysel. Lela would have been a much better parent and he never should have taken her. Being just a baby herself at age fourteen and a half and ready to give birth, she still didn't know how it would exit. She truly believed that God just decided to make her a mother, and she felt special and blessed that He had done so. Little did she know the baby growing inside her had actually come from Wannie.

Maysel was still thankful that John's anger towards her was under control and hadn't lasted beyond the evening when he realized that she was not "just gittin fat." It was obvious that he wanted to kill someone for impregnating Maysel. Following that night, loud and heavy arguing between John and Nettie could be heard coming from inside the cabin at night. Their arguments were like powerful thunderstorms: loud and scary, sometimes taking an agonizingly long time to blow over, but causing little apparent damage. Nettie had been very instrumental in calming John by assuring him that killing someone would only make matters worse and would change nothing. There was another reason for her concern. Wannie was Nettie's brother and she wanted to protect him from John's wrath. As if not discussing things would make them go away, John ignored the entire issue. He never mentioned Maysel's condition again. He hated for his comfort zone to be interrupted in any way.

Her belly now very closely resembled Mr. Clay's and had "dropped." This meant that delivery time was close. The unborn child was very active and Maysel was ready to unload the burden of being pregnant. Her feet stayed swollen, the pressure in her pelvic region was strong and her back hurt. She waddled to maneuver herself around. It was about time for the magic to begin. Keeping a close watch on her belly button, Maysel waited anxiously to see how this would transpire. She was still in the dark concerning the childbirth process.

It was Friday and, of course, John was away on "business." One would think that he would want to be around for the birth of his grandchild, but no, no, no, not John. He was such a coward that he deliberately planned his absence from this event. Mrs. Hagerman had been observing Maysel's progress, and after seeing John's car leave the hollow, she went directly to the cabin. Upon her arrival, she discovered that Maysel had been having very hard "cramps" this morning. Maysel blamed the cramping on the beans she had eaten the night before.

"They've never cramped me before like this." Maysel had said. "And I feel so plugged up too, Mrs. Hagerman." Maysel thought she was constipated. How innocent.

Mrs. Hagerman knew these "cramps" were the beginning of labor pains and quickly left the cabin, telling Maysel that she would be back soon. It didn't matter that it was Friday and the weekend was coming up, Maysel would need a doctor before this day was up. In about one hour, she returned with Doc Hatfield. By now, Maysel's "cramps" were very hard and getting closer and closer together. This meant nothing to Maysel, but did give Doc a clue about when the baby would come.

Doc Hatfield's hair was vaguely camel-colored and had fallen out on the top, leaving a pale blonde ring of hair around the crown of his head. On his nose rested a small pair of wire-framed glasses. Half the time, he looked over the top of them instead of through them. He had an air about him that just required respect, and it was always given. Maysel didn't like it, but he examined her and began preparing to deliver the baby. He told Mrs. Hagerman to put some water on the stove and find some rags. Aware that Maysel had no rags, the teacher had brought some with her. Doc sat his little bag on the table and emptied its contents of implements onto a cloth that he obtained from the bag. This didn't look like too much of a job to him. He just had to wait and nature would probably do the rest. He had delivered many, many babies in his life as a doctor, and he felt confident that this would be an easy delivery.

Doc had been there about three hours and Maysel's pains were coming harder and harder. She would catch her breath, clench her teeth and try again. Her face would turn blue each time, but she still didn't know what this was all about. With each pain, Mrs. Hagerman would say, "You can do it now, a little more, a little more. You're doin fine, just fine."

Five hours later, Maysel's suffering seemed extreme and she was in the midst of dangerous complications. Of what nature, Doc didn't know, but his instincts told him that something wasn't quite right. She heaved her body with such force that she almost rolled off the bed several times, insisting that the being within her would surely rip her apart. This was torturous pain that she could not endure. She feared she could not live.

"I can't do this, I can't do this! God! I *cannot* do this!" she wailed. Her sobs were very loud, long and filled with despair. She prayed.

The baby's head was in view, but Maysel's condition had deteriorated. Her respiration was too shallow. She was pale, weak and becoming unable to participate in the birth of her own child. She was completely delirious. Exhausted, she gave in to one more contraction and giving it everything she had left, she squealed and groaned and struggled with the pain. Doc had no way of knowing that eclampsia had occurred. When blood pressure elevates very high and very fast, then suddenly drops drastically low, the patient is brought to convulsions, often resulting in death. Someone usually dies, the mother, the baby or both. It is uncommon for both to survive.

As if shot by a gun, her head fell back on the bed. Her fluttering eyes rolled back in her head and her body began to convulse as if she were having an epileptic seizure. Moments later, the jerking stopped. She had lost consciousness. Her body collapsed and became pale, limp and lifeless. There was no breathing and no sign of life. This situation had escalated to a very serious and critical level. Tension filled the room and the stillness seemed to last a great while, but considering the quantity of tension, the incident may have lasted only seconds. Not to say that someone did something wrong, but sometimes women die in childbirth, just like sometimes people get sick and die. Thank God it doesn't happen very often, but it happens.

Being without the extensive safety net of modern medicine, Doc had only a few instruments with which to work and no drugs. Even so, he knew what was required of him. He must try to save the baby. He always hated to deliver a dead baby. He viewed them as little stillborn persons, with souls, gone to Heaven far too prematurely and denied the privilege of experiencing a world larger than a womb. This made him want to cry for the babies, as well as the parents. At that very moment, he wept as thoughts of losing Maysel went through his mind. It was these type things that would bring Doc Hatfield down for days. He hated losing anybody to death, especially a young person. Dripping from his face like summer rain from the roof edge, his sweat could not be distinguished from his tears.

With only moments to act and with the assistance of Mrs. Hagerman, he forced the baby from the birth canal. It was blue from prolonged lack of oxygen. Quickly tying and cutting the cord, he struggled to bring life into the small, blue, limp body. Their backs were toward Maysel as they vigorously worked. Finally, Doc grinned, sighed loudly and took a deep breath. The teacher smiled and threw her hands over her chest in amazement as the sounds of the crying baby filled the room. It would live. Mrs. Hagerman prepared a pan of warm water and began cleaning the baby girl. She was the most amazingly beautiful thing ever. Since there was no scales on which to weigh her, Doc guessed her weight to be about eight pounds, a very large baby for someone the age and size of Maysel to deliver. She had tiny rolls of baby fat on her arms that gave the appearance of little bracelets at her wrists. Her tiny nose resembled a gentle ski jump and with the exception of a few downy dark blonde hairs, she was bald, yet adorable. She was a survivor. She had already been in a fight with death, had won and was still fighting.

Their attention still focused on the baby and their backs toward Maysel, they heard a very loud moan. Doc Hatfield's eyes grew to the size of saucers and he just stared. He couldn't believe his ears. "Oh . . . my . . . God!" He whispered. "She's not dead!" Closing his eyes, as if afraid to look, he managed to softly say, "How bad did I tear her up?

He swiftly turned around and ran to Maysel's side. Judging from the bloody bedclothes, she had suffered a great loss of blood and her chances of survival were slim, but he had to try to save her. This was a miracle, one like he had never witnessed before. Finding Maysel groaning and breathing, he could hardly contain the happiness he felt. Her respiration was much better and she gained consciousness within the hour. A big smile was on his face as he rushed to assist Maysel. He patched her up the best he could and hoped for the best. "She'll make it," he thought, "she just has to." He prayed. Of course she would. Remember God's promise to Lela?

Later, opening her eyes, and seeing only darkness, Maysel thought it was the middle of the night and that there was no light in the room. Doc and Mrs. Hagerman continued their words of encouragement. They told her about her beautiful, healthy baby girl. They praised her and told her how well she had done.

"What happened? Maysel asked. "I was crampin' real bad and all of a sudden, I went to sleep or something." She said weakly. "A girl." She sighed as she closed her eyes seemingly to get more strength.

Doc and Mrs. Hagerman busied themselves in an effort to clean up the mess created by the day's history. Bloody rags and bedding had to be bagged and laundered. The waste from the birth needed to be disposed of and Maysel still was in need of cleaning. Mrs. Hagerman prepared another pan of warm water and proceeded to help Doc clean her body and change the bedding. Loss of blood had left Maysel in an extremely weakened state. Doc encouraged her to rest.

Clean up was done and Doc prepared to leave. He wanted to check on his patient one more time before leaving. Making certain that she was still in a conscious state, he took Maysel's hand and while patting it, called her name a time or two.

Maysel opened her eyes and appeared to be staring at the ceiling. "Why are we in the dark? Can't one of ya light the oil lamp? We need some light in here. It's dark."

A look of fear came over Doc's face and he passed his hand back and forth in front of Maysel's eyes. She just stared. There was no evidence that she could see. It appeared that Maysel had lost her eyesight. Tears filled Mrs. Hagerman's eyes as she realized the truth. "Oh, God," she thought, "how much worse can this be?

There was no way around it. Doc had to tell Maysel the truth. Looking away so he wouldn't break down and cry, he said, "Maysel, you had a really rough time with this. There was a time there when we thought we lost you, but you made it, and you'll make it through this too."

"Make it through what? "

"I hate like the devil to tell you this, but . . . it's not dark in here . . . I'm afraid you're blind." He said. There was no other way of telling her. "I'm hopin' it's temporary, but it could be permanent. We have to wait a few weeks to see. Ya never know how these things will go."

Trying to look around, Maysel panicked, and she began to cry and sob. She had little strength left and this piece of information was almost more than she could bear. She almost wished she had died. Her life didn't seem worth living. Then, she thought of her baby. In between sobs, she cried, "I can't even *see* my baby, let alone take *care* of her." In helpless despair, she sank back and cried herself to sleep, not caring if she ever woke up again.

Doc left and Mrs. Hagerman spent the night with Maysel. Sitting in a chair beside the bed she wanted to be there each time Maysel awoke or stirred, so that she could give the pitiful young woman some water. Her heart ached for Maysel and she prayed all night that God would sustain her and make things well and good.

Chapter 29

Early the next morning, Wannie showed up at the cabin. If he was appalled by what he saw when he entered the room, he kept his disappointment to himself. Maysel was indeed glad to hear his footsteps, although she could not see him. They did not speak yet. He wrapped his arms around her shoulders and pulled her to him and gave her a kiss on the lips as gentle as the first one they had shared a year earlier. He took a few deep breaths to try and calm himself and to settle his stomach, which was very upset from the reality of John's abandonment of Maysel. Mrs. Hagerman told him of Maysel's blindness and what a weakened state she was in. She had spent most of the night in a fog, neither here nor there. He was devastated. With a look if bewilderment on his face, he just rocked Maysel for a long time, a swaying motion that just seemed right for the moment. She pressed her forehead against his chest and it was apparent that Wannie, like Maysel had absolutely no idea of how much responsibility would soon come to rest on their young, unprepared shoulders. Looking at Mrs. Hagerman, he could tell that she was exhausted and needed to be relieved. He announced that he would stay and care for Maysel and the baby. Just sixteen, but he was the only help available. During the conversation, it was mentioned that John would be gone indefinitely, which made Wannie feel safe and more comfortable about staying. Even as a small child, Wannie kept his distance from John. For some reason, the man made him nervous.

"Mrs. Hagerman," Wannie said. "I promise that I'll take care of them. Don't worry. I *will* take care of them." The sincerity and determination in his voice let Mrs. Hagerman believe that he was telling the truth. Guessing Wannie to be the father, but never asking confirmation, she complied and went home for some much-needed rest. It had been a long twenty-four hours.

Wannie looked around at the situation. Maysel was in bed; the baby was in a wooden box wrapped in a blanket, asleep. Assuming the major responsibility of all this, he didn't quite know where to start. He began by quietly re-building the fire. He prepared some potatoes in a pot of water on top of the pot-bellied stove to make soup.

Maysel stirred and Wannie rushed to her side to hold her hand. "I'm here," he said softly. You're gonna be O.K., I promise."

"Wannie, I can't see."

"I know, but I'm here and you're gonna be alright."

"I don't know what I'm gonna do if I can't see how to take care of the baby. Why would God give me a baby and then let me be blind. I don't understand."

"I'll help you. We'll get through this together. We're tough. We'll make it." He said confidently. Although in his mind, he didn't see how this could happen.

Just then the baby began to cry. He noticed a stack of flour sack diapers left by Mrs. Hagerman on the table. He took one and used it on the baby. He laid the baby in Maysel's arms and she held it to her leaking breast. Immediately, the crying was replaced by the grunting sounds of the suckling baby.

Wannie made egg sandwiches on some biscuits that he had brought with him. He knew there would be a need for food. He was making a fine start. Dinner was cooking, the baby was diapered and fed, and the mother was about to eat breakfast. Wannie was proud of his performance so far and Maysel was more than proud of him. What would she do without him? What *would* she do?

Wannie stayed the rest of the day and did a few things to make things easier. A clothesline for drying diapers was fashioned by driving nails into the walls and stretching a piece of twine from one wall to the other behind the stove. The table, rocking chair and bed were placed closer together and moved near the stove. After a long discussion, a plan was made and the two of them executed it together. There was no other choice. They must survive, and so, they did.

Wannie came every morning and kept the fire going. He brought whatever food he could find for Maysel. He did everything he could to prepare them for the rest of the day. On the right side of the rocking chair, in the floor, he placed a flour sack full of fresh diapers and on the left side there was an empty sack for the soiled ones. In the evening, Wannie washed the soiled ones and hung them on the clothesline behind the stove to dry. Maysel sat in darkness and breast fed the baby, sang and rocked it in the chair whenever she was not on the bed trying to recover. Getting used to being blind was not easy. She had practiced moving from the chair to the bed and back to the chair, while holding Lela Mae (named after each of their mothers) in her arms. Wannie made her prove to him that she could do it in his absence.

He spent the night as often as he could, but if not possible, he came early in the morning and later in the evening to carry out his part of the plan. What a trooper he was. He had displayed the dedication of a saint through all of this. Poppy's leaving at this most crucial time did not improve Maysel's situation any and it certainly didn't win him a drop of respect from Wannie or anyone else for that matter. Wannie almost hated him. What a louse!

Lela Mae was now seven weeks old and was growing considerably. Mrs. Hagerman visited about once a week and it was her day to check in on them. She always praised and commended Wannie for the impeccable job he was doing. His dedication to Maysel and Lela Mae was unparalleled.

Arriving early, Mrs. Hagerman headed straight to see how Lela Mae was doing. One would have thought the baby was her grandchild from the way she looked at it. Maysel and Lela Mae were still asleep and Wannie was busy doing his routine morning chores. Hearing Mrs. Hagerman's footsteps, Maysel opened her eyes and yawned. "Wannie," she said, "Wannie, are you here? What's this? She could see *light! Light*! For the first time in seven weeks, she could see *light*! Everything was blurry, but she could see *light!*

"I'm here." Wannie said as he walked toward the bed.

"Wannie, come here." She said with a surprised look on her face. She reached for him with both hands and pulled his face closer to her own. Looking closely and running her shaking fingers across his face, she could see his blurred image. Mrs. Hagerman moved closer to the bed to be sure that she was hearing correctly.

"I can see! Oh, my God! I can see! Not very good, but I can *see!*" She exclaimed. Tears stung Wannie's eyes and looking across the bed at Mrs. Hagerman, he saw the stream of tears rolling down the face of the woman who had been so kind and supportive to Maysel. He was grateful to her beyond words and was glad that she was present to witness this triumphant event.

"Are you sure? Wannie wanted confirmation. "Are you *sure*? Can you see me? He asked again.

"Not good, but yes, I can see you and you're the first thing I wanted to see." Turning her head, she smiled at her baby. "Besides this of course." She kissed Lela Mae on the forehead.

Not meaning to ignore Mrs. Hagerman, Maysel reached her free arm out to embrace the guardian angel that had been her mentor since she was six and one half years old. This wonderful woman had guided Maysel as if she were her very own daughter. Whatever good that Maysel may be, she owed it to this lady who had taught her so much and who was by her side during those dark hours when she was presumed dead.

Crying as she hugged Mrs. Hagerman, Maysel said, "I don't know how to begin to thank you. God must surely have placed you in this hollow just for me. I'd sure be dead by now if it wasn't for you. Thank you so much."

"You're so welcome Maysel. Why, I never would have had a daughter if you hadn't come along, now would I? Mrs. Hagerman said. Her eyes and her heart always seemed to smile. Maysel loved her.

Chapter 30

*T*he Great Depression was devastating the country and people were struggling daily just to survive from one day to the next. In rural areas of West Virginia, malnutrition was great and money was almost non-existent. People usually grew their own food and animals, or worked for food. Bartering each other for services was also a popular means of survival. Families lived in the neediest of conditions. Wannie's family was no different. Since his father had died tragically when he was only ten years old, it was presumed that Wannie (being the eldest son) would take the responsibility for meeting the family's needs. So young, yet this massive burden was placed on his shoulders and he had heroically carried it for more than six years. Adding to that equation was his love for Maysel, who also had needs. Although she had John (or did she?), Wannie still wanted to know that her and the baby's needs were met. This was an enormous load for an adult, let alone a teen-ager. Things were getting worse and something had to be done.

In the spring of 1938 Wannie joined the Civilian

Conservation Corps (CCC), a program put into effect by the Franklin D. Roosevelt administration. It had been in effect for five years and was designed to give relief to single, unemployed young men (ages 17-25) who were capable of doing physical labor. Their enrollment period was six months, but could be reinstated after that. It was a public work relief program, which focused on natural resource conservation. The young men lived in camps, wore uniforms and lived under quasi-military discipline. Very few had more than a year of high school education: few had work experience beyond occasional odd jobs and farm work. This was a training station designed to teach these young men to build parks, help restore forests, build recreation facilities, save land from erosion and help to restore watersheds that provided clean water. Each enrollee received $30.00 a month and each month $25.00 of that was sent home to their parents. Wannie's mother (Mae) was the recipient of his allotment. The other $5.00 they got to keep for their own use. His housing, food and clothing were provided by the program. The young men lived in tents while building their barracks. Each camp eventually contained several different kinds of buildings for living and working.

Wannie arrived at the CC Camps and soon found himself working very hard, but he was conditioned to hard work and didn't mind it. Having a very likable personality he soon became very popular among his comrades. He fit in well. Life was simple and everyone worked hard, but it wasn't without fun. Sporting events, music, baseball, boxing, Saturday night dances, and education were among the most popular recreational past times. He learned to drive and learned how to use common building tools. Wannie could sing well and was very musically inclined. He learned to play guitar in the CC Camps and participated in boxing events, which he loved. Win or lose, Wannie was always a good sport.

After a few weeks in the CC Camps, the enrollees could take short leaves. The nearby town of Pineville, West Virginia was where most of them went. It was here that the young men were introduced to alcoholic beverages. Not a pretty sight to see on Sunday afternoon. About 25 young men with hangovers in one place provided entertainment to those who had not indulged. Headaches, vomiting and heaving was plentiful following that first leave pass. A lesson well learned for Wannie. He wanted no more of that and was very careful not to enter that level of intoxication again for a long time to come. The next leave he took was to see his family and Maysel.

He had been in the CC Camps almost six months when Wannie was given the announcement of his mother's death. The cause of death was unknown, but Wannie always suspected that she died from tuberculosis. Mae was a kind and helpful woman. Neighbors could always expect her to be present in time of need, no matter what the case may be. Wannie must have inherited his sense of dedication from her. She was a widow and was known to entertain male friends, but that doesn't make you worthless. She never professed Christianity, but she had a heart of gold.

Attending her funeral were the hollow residents and her children, who all gathered at the cemetery. Wannie's sisters were all married by now and his younger brother Coy (who never married), had been living with a neighboring couple who finished rearing him. The only sibling remaining without a parent was Walter. They called him, "Junior" or "June" for short. At the time of Mae's death he was 13 years old and far too young to care for himself. He would make his home with Wannie.

Wannie's mother had always been kind to Maysel and had been a source of food many times during her young life. She loved Mae and her death saddened Maysel. She held her baby and accompanied Wannie as he stood near his mother's open grave. He had a broken heart and a feeling of helplessness. Gazing down into the open cavity he watched the shabby, homemade, thin, pine box containing his mother's body being lowered into it. There were cracks in the box and he had future nightmares of water entering it and dripping onto her body. They could not afford the materials for a coffin, just a box. His heart ached and his head was spinning. He thought he would surely pass out, but didn't. He loved his mother dearly and the fact that poverty prevented him from giving his mother a decent burial would haunt him for the rest of his life. That horrible memory would stay vivid in his mind forever.

Wannie pulled himself together and remained in the CC Camps for a few more months. He decided that circumstances required him to be discharged. Both parents were deceased and his 13-year-old brother

Junior needed care and supervision. His allotment check was being sent home and Maysel was caring for Junior, but serious decisions needed to be made and made fast. After a lot of thought, Wannie had a plan and the first part of that plan was that he must leave the CC Camps.

He made the request for discharge, signed the necessary papers and waited for them to be processed before heading home.

Chapter 31

Sam Hurley had been one of Wannie's best friends during his stay in the CC Camps and he hated leaving him. The two had worked and played together since the first day of Camp. One of Sam's family members owned a car and Sam made arrangements for them to drive Wannie home. He was all packed up and threw his belongings into the car. Standing there to say good-bye to Sam was a sad occasion, but Wannie had serious responsibilities at home and had no other choice. They had worked and played very hard. Together, they learned that life has some interests besides work. They had a brief conversation of good-bye and shook hands, hoping that they would see each other soon. That didn't happen until a number of years later.

The CC Camp had given Wannie a new outlook on life. He had learned enough from this experience to fill a small book. While there, one thing he learned from the other young men was conception. Yep, "the birds and the bees." When first told, it seemed to Wannie that they were making it all up. Then, it finally dawned on him, it was truth. Now, all the pieces fit and all his questions were answered. It now made sense. God *did* give Maysel a baby (as she believed), but He had used Wannie to help with it. Why had no one from the hollow ever told him about this? He now had it all figured out. He was a father. Lela Mae was just as much a part of him as she was of Maysel. Wow! That was awesome. He couldn't wait to educate Maysel on this subject. Unbelievably, she knew less than he did about such things and she needed to be informed.

The drive to Laurel Branch Hollow was about two hours long. The roads were not paved and speed was limited. While passing through the small town of Oceana, West Virginia, Wannie's attention was caught by a sign that said: "Coal Miners Needed. Apply Within."

"Hey," Wannie said, "do you mind stopping for a minute so I can go in and talk to them about a job?

"Not at all," the driver said as he pulled over and let Wannie out of the car.

"I'll just be a minute. Thanks." He said as he hurried toward the door.

It was a small company store and the man he needed to speak with was seated behind bars that resembled a bank teller's station. Peering through the bars at Wannie, the bald man asked, "Can I help ya?"

"I seen your sign and I'd like to be a coal miner." Wannie said.

"How old are ya? The man asked.

"I'm eighteen." He lied. "I just left the CC Camps and I need a job."

"Well, it's good that you're eighteen, cause that's how old ya gotta be for hirin'." The man announced. "We won't be hirin nobody for two weeks though. That's when the next half starts. If you come back then, we'll probably put you to work. It pays $1.50 a day. This here's the company store. If you need to buy somethin' and we sell it here, ya gotta buy it from us. Understand? He said sternly as if it were the law.

"I do." Wannie said as he hurried back to his ride home. "A dollar and a half a day! What I could do with that much money! We could leave the hollow!"

Returning to the car, Wannie's head was full of happiness and dreams of getting his family (yes, his family) out of the hollow and away from John Brunty. He rode in silence the rest of the way home trying to get it straight in his head how this would transpire.

Finally home, Wannie removed his belongings from the car and politely thanked the people for being so nice to give him a lift home. He would have invited them in, but there was no one there at the time and he had no way of knowing what to expect inside the house. The car left a cloud of dust and Wannie entered the house for the first time since his mother's death. He experienced a feeling of loneliness like none he had ever known. Although the sparse furnishings were still there and looked familiar, the place seemed cold and empty. Growing up, there had always been noise coming from the McCarty home. Mae was a very noisy person, as were all the other family members. The silence was deafening and he longed to hear his mother's voice. He now knew how Maysel must have felt when she was taken from her mother at age five. Losing your mother gives one a feeling of disconnection that only comes with this event.

"June!" He yelled. "Junior! Where are you? Going to the back door, he opened it and yelled again, "June! Are you here? There was no answer.

Closing the door and returning inside, Wannie figured that June must be with Maysel. If he was, then he would be in the presence of John Brunty. How would that be goin? This was too much. He had to leave this tomb and would not return until another human being was with him.

He began his walk toward the Brunty cabin. Arriving, he knocked on the door. June opened it.

"June, is John home? He asked.

"No, he's been gone since day before yesterday." June answered.

He gently moved June aside and stepped inside and found Maysel and Lela Mae. The reunion was quite overwhelming and lasted about five minutes. They hugged, they kissed, they asked questions, and neither could talk fast enough. John was not expected back until the next day, so Wannie spent the night with Maysel.

"When Poppy's here, he acts like the baby and I ain't even here." Maysel said. "He has never held her and he won't even look at her. I don't know what's the matter with him. He was gone for about two months when Lela Mae was born and when he come back, he didn't seem happy to see us at all. I don't understand."

Wannie understood. He understood all too well.

John Brunty left Maysel to have her baby alone and
with no plans for her delivery. He was absent from
her delivery and was gone for two months following.
Maysel was worthless to John now that she was a
mother. She couldn't work and be as productive as
she had in the past. Wannie added all these factors
up and there was only one answer to this riddle. John
had left Maysel and her unborn child in the head of a
hollow, alone and without help-to die! That's it and
Wannie was certain of that. The thought infuriated
him. To spare Maysel's feelings, he never mentioned
his suspicions to her.

To confirm his employment with the coalmine,
Wannie revisited the company store. It had been five
days since his first visit. He explained his situation to
the boss and was told that he could report to work in
nine days. It was official. He had a job. He located a
two-room house in Oceana. It was barely furnished,
but it would serve its purpose until better could be
done. They just needed a place to live. At any rate, it
was better living arrangements than Maysel had been
living in for the past 10 years in the hollow with John.
He paid the rent and had the power turned on. No
oil lamps. That was a real convenience, which didn't
exist in the hollow. He was given all the information
concerning his new job and went back to the hollow
to tell Maysel.

Rushing home with the good news, Wannie was
finally filled with hope that this would end their life-
long nightmare in the hollow. He and June stayed
at the McCarty house and away from John's cabin.
Wannie and Maysel planned to get married and finish

rearing June, but that plan had an obstacle . . . John. Wannie was ready to take his family with him out of the hollow, with or without John's blessings. One way or the other, they *were* leaving!

Early the next morning, Wannie was awakened by the sound of John's car driving by on his way home. Today, he would confront John about their plans and face any challenge that went with it. He waited about thirty minutes, checked to make sure the shotgun was loaded and propped it up behind the door.

"June, stay in the house until I get back. Do you hear me? Don't come out the house. I mean it. There might be trouble and you need to stay safe inside this house." He said, as he left and walked toward the Brunty cabin.

Stepping upon the porch as he had so many other times in his life, Wannie was very nervous, but sometimes you just gotta do whatcha gotta do. He knocked on the door, and John came to the door. "What do *you* want? He asked as if talking to an insect.

"Come out here Mr. Brunty, I need to talk to you a few minutes." Wannie said.

John came out on the porch. To make it difficult for John to re-enter the house, Wannie stepped between him and the door.

"I asked you what you wanted." John said in a hateful tone of voice.

"I've come for my family, Mr.Brunty." Wannie said in his kindest voice.

"Boy, are you lost or drunk? Your family lives in the McCarty house right over there. This is my house and *you* ain't family." John snarled.

"I'm talking about Maysel and Lela Mae. Mr. Brunty, I've been in the CC Camps for several months and I've learned a lot of stuff-stuff that should have been told to me when I was about twelve years old. I know that Lela Mae is just as much a part of me as she is a part of Maysel. She is *ours*. *They* are *my* family and I've come to get them."

"I don't think so." John snickered as if to doubt Wannie's sanity.

"I've got a job and a place for us to live. I'm gonna tell ya this just once again. I've come to get my family. *This* is the way it is," his voice was almost a whisper. "If there's a drop of decency in you, you'll drive me and Maysel to Bluewell, Virginia to get married. You can sign that she is old enough. I hope that's what ya do. And if ya don't, I'm *still* gonna take them outa here . . . *after* I blow your head off your shoulders with a 410 shotgun on your way out of this hollow. I hate your guts and I've got plenty of reasons to feel the way I do. Just give me one more reason. That's all I need, just one more. Got the picture? You'll have to pass *me* on your way out. It's a mile outa here. You can't stay in this cabin forever."

"Boy, don't come up here and threaten me you little snot."

Staring coldly at John, Wannie continued, "I *will* do it. And then, I'll take my family. By the way, don't try nothin dumb. Right now, a friend of mine is sittin' in the woods with your chest in the sights of his gun ready to blow a hole in you big enough to throw a gallon jug of moonshine through." He bluffed.

"You've got a lot of enemies and so many people would love to see you dead that they'd never prove who did it. They probably wouldn't even want to. Now, what'll it be? He meant it, and John knew it.

John's face was pale as a ghost. Trying to save face, he pretended to think it through. Everything had always been about John and his comfort zone. He didn't even like to cut himself while shaving, let alone to be blown away by a sniper. Besides, Maysel could no longer work as hard for him. She had a dern young'un to occupy her time and that meant that he now had two mouths to feed and neither of them were productive. This might be a good deal for him.

"Well, it looks like there's gonna be a weddin." John said in defeat (something he hated). "When do ya wanna go? He asked with a "have-it-your-way" look on his face.

"The sooner the better, we've got a lot to do before I go to work in the coal mines in a few days. Thank you Mr. Brunty." He said as he stuck his head through the door and announced that the weddin' would be tomorrow. He nodded his head at John and left without extending his visit. He had said what he intended to say and he didn't want to push it.

Chapter 32

Maysel's heart leaped in her chest after Wannie's announcement that they would be getting married tomorrow. It didn't matter to her about the short notice. Taking a deep breath and kissing Lela Mae on the forehead, she began to collect her thoughts. They had no money to spend on a wedding, so she would just do the best she could. Looking down at herself, she realized that her only clothing was the bib overalls, tee shirt and high-top leather shoes. No bride should be wearing this. But, even if it meant wearing the overalls, she was willing to marry Wannie under any circumstances.

"Wait," She thought, "I do have a dress." She announced to John (she didn't ask, he could just get used to it) that she was going to Mrs. Hagerman's house for a few minutes and would return whenever she was through. "I have to take care of something." She said, and out the door she went carrying her baby.

Mrs. Hagerman opened the door and greeted Maysel with a big hug.

"Mrs. Hagerman," Maysel beamed, "we're

gittin' married tomorrow, Wannie and me. We leave for Bluewell Virginia in the morning. Poppy's gonna sign for me." She said proudly almost blushing. "I need a favor from you. I ain't got a weddin' dress and I need to borrow one of the dresses you fixed for me, if it's alright. I'll be careful not to hurt it and I'll give it right back to you as soon as we git back."

"Oh Maysel, how wonderful! I'll do anything I can to help. You know I will." And with the excitement of a teen-ager, she ushered Maysel into her house. Chattering non-stop, she continued, "I think you should wear the lighter colored one, you know the cream colored one. I have a pair of shoes that matches it. You can wear those. Oh, and I can roll your hair with rags tonight so it can curl while you sleep and I'll comb it out for you in the morning. I'm gonna give you some of my undies, and . . ." on and on she went with one statement running into the other as she dashed about trying to get this bride together.

The next morning, Wannie prepared himself for the big day. He had learned how to practice personal hygiene from the CC Camps and began shaving his face. He hoped this day would go smoothly and that there would be no ugly confrontations with John today. He'd hate to kill John, but, the chilling truth is, he *would* if necessary. His wedding apparel was a light blue shirt and blue jeans, which had been given to him by the CC Camps. It was the best he had.

Maysel had risen very early that morning and made her way to Mrs. Hagerman's house. She had a lot to do before they left. She would be a bride today . . . not a brute. Leaving Mrs. Hagerman's house that morning, Maysel looked radiant. The cream-colored dress was perfect for her and fit her well. Mrs. Hagerman had done a beautiful job with Maysel's hair. It was wavy and hung on her shoulders. The finishing touch was a spray of Mrs. Hagerman's perfume. Wow! Wannie would be surprised. In addition, the teacher had filled a bag and handed it to Maysel. "This is yours. I want you to have these things because you deserve them." Looking inside Maysel found all three dresses that Mrs. Hagerman had altered to fit her and shoes to match them, one handkerchief and a small testament to carry at her wedding. Maysel was touched and elated. The two women embraced each other and Maysel went home to join Wannie and John.

Wannie and Junior bravely stepped onto the porch of John's cabin. Not knowing what to expect, Wannie made cautious observations in doing so. John walked out onto the porch and asked Wannie if he was ready. He seemed in good spirits, but Wannie wondered if it was false.

"Ready as I'll ever be." Wannie answered, as he looked up into the woods making implications that his gunman friend was watching.

Maysel came out carrying Lela Mae and the sight of her took Wannie's breath away. He had never seen her in a dress before. To him, she was the most beautiful woman on earth and the look on his face confirmed that he was pleased at what he saw.

He reached for Lela Mae and as they made their way to the car, Wannie was instructing Junior to stay at home all day. "You are thirteen. You're old enough to stay home by yourself until we git back this evening.

Don't go out of the yard. Behave yourself and don't bother the neighbors, ya hear me? He ordered as he got into the car. "If ya git hungry, there's soup on the stove. We'll be back this evening." He patted his younger brother on the shoulder and the car took them from the hollow.

Processing the paper work seemed to take an eternity. They had been at the Court House for more than 45 minutes and were very nervous and anxious. Maysel was barely 15 and they feared her age would be questioned. Finally, their names were called and they received their marriage license along with instructions to the nearest Justice of the Peace. You'd think John would hold Lela Mae long enough for the ceremony to take place, but he didn't offer. In Maysel's hand was the testament and handkerchief and in Wannie's arms was Lela Mae. "This is my little maid of honor." Maysel said with a smile and kiss. The ceremony was short and within a matter of minutes, they were married.

The trip back to Laurel Branch Hollow was a quiet one. Only the baby sounds from Lela Mae's voice could be heard. She had been exceptionally good today and Maysel could not believe it.

That night, John spent the night alone in the cabin for the first time since his return to Laurel Branch and the newly-formed family of Wannie, Maysel, Lela Mae and Junior lodged at the McCarty house. The "family" would move to Oceana within the next few days and their lives together would begin. Oh yeah, Maysel had not been visited by "Aunt Flow" since Wannie had visited while on leave almost three months ago.

Chapter 33

Riding a bus was very noisy and uncomfortable and cigarette smokers made it even worse, but Lela Trout had become accustomed to it. The frequent stops, the wind blowing through the windows and crying babies were other things that tried her patience when she traveled. The smell of the exhaust fumes was sickening and if the road had many curves in it, she experienced motion sickness. She had boarded many, many buses during her seventeen-year search for Maysel. Buses had carried her to one dead end after another, but she never stopped searching and still was trusting God to fulfill His promise to her (that she *would* see Maysel again).

Looking out the window of the bus, she thought about how Jack had been so kind, compassionate and thoughtful each time she left him to investigate a lead about where she might find Maysel. He was truly a guardian angel. No one in the entire world could have been more supportive of her. She was convinced that God Himself had placed Jack and Edwin in her life. She loved them both deeply, but her life would never be complete without finding Maysel.

She had spent years in search of a girl with the unusual name of Maysel. Many leads in the past had led to nothing. This one seemed more promising because it had Maysel's name attached to it. The information came from Kate Barber, an old friend of Lela's. Kate's in-laws lived in Oceana, West Virginia and had made acquaintance with a young lady by the name Maysel who was about twenty-two years of age. If no other lead was followed-up on . . . this one *would* be. Lela was in Oceana to check it out. Lela no longer carried the photo of five-year-old Maysel with her. After seventeen years, it was unlikely that anyone would recognize her from the photo.

Roads were not yet paved and the bus left a cloud of dust as it came into Oceana.

She coughed as a puff of dust came through the window at her. Just then, a drizzle of rain began to fall and Lela was thankful for it. It didn't last long, but it did control the dust. Only one main street existed and smaller dirt roads branched off from it to small neighborhoods. There wasn't much to see here. Looking down the streets as she passed them, Lela noticed how much the small homes resembled the ones in her area. They passed a few small businesses, a few modest houses, a small grocery store, a church, one gas station and coming up on the left was Bean's Store, a small mercantile. The bus came to a stop in front of it and Lela stepped off.

Her mouth was dry and she had visions of drinking an orange-flavored drink. Maybe they had one in there. She entered the store and immediately came in contact with the smell of "new" things like shoes, dresses, fabric, and an assortment of various items. As she browsed, she couldn't help but notice the clerks staring at her. Both of them tried not to, but they were staring. Whatever were they thinking? Did they think she looked suspicious? Were they expecting her to steal? What?

"May I help you? One of them finally asked.

"I need something to drink and maybe you can help me with some information." Lela said. She selected a drink, set it up on the counter and paid for it. After taking a big satisfying drink from the cold bottle, she said, "Thank you." The clerks were still trying not to stare at her, but were having a difficult time doing so.

"I'm looking for a young lady about twenty-two years old by the name of Maysel and I heard she may be living here in Oceana. Can you help me with that? She's my missing daughter and I've been searching for her for seventeen years." Lela recited the description as she had at least one hundred times.

"The reason we can't take our eyes off you is because you look so much like Maysel McCarty that lives on the back street. We just can't get over it." One of the ladies said, still staring at Lela.

"Can you tell me how to get there? I'll walk." Lela said.

"Sure," They began giving her directions to where Maysel lived.

The three of them walked outside in front of the store and one of them pointed down the street, which led down the side of the store. "Walk down this street until you come to the last street, then and turn right.

Maysel and Wannie live in the fourth house on the left. You can't miss it." She kindly said.

"Thank you. Thank you so, so much." Lela said with heart-felt gratitude. She started walking so fast that she feared falling down. Could this be it? Could this be my Maysel? After all these years, could this be it? Could this long search finally be over? Lela's excitement could not be measured at this point. She had never had such a good lead. She prayed, "Dear God, please let it be, *please* let it be Maysel."

Chapter 34

Lela was a nervous wreck, shaking even. Could this be the moment that she had dreamed of for more than seventeen years? Could this really be the moment when God's promise to her would be fulfilled? Could this long, painful chapter in her life be closed today? It had almost killed her. Would this day end the searching, the crying, the endless aching inside and could it end the mental torment of having one's only child missing? Could all the emotional hell that she had endured end today?

How many twenty-two-year-old girls could there possibly be in this area by the name of Maysel? Lela herself had never heard the name but one other time. What would she say to her? How would she know for sure if this girl is her? Could she touch her? Could she hold her? Will she know me? These and other countless questions ran through Lela's head so fast that her head seemed to spin. Never being this close to finding Maysel, she was consumed by an excitement so strong that the burning tension was painful. It seemed to burn her flesh.   •

Standing on the corner where she was to turn

right, Lela paused. Was she ready for this? She turned right and went a few more steps in the direction of the designated house. Stopping dead in her tracks, she desperately needed to compose herself. "If this is for real, I can't fall apart now. What's wrong with me? She thought as she took in a very deep breath and slowly exhaled.

"God, you said you'd be my strength and I need some of that strength right now." She prayed as she strained her eyes looking down the narrow, unpaved street hoping to see someone. In front of three of the houses were cars parked parallel to the fences, but she saw no one. It was as if the entire neighborhood was away on vacation. She noticed a lazy-looking dog lying in the middle of the road. "I hope he's friendly. All I need right now is for a dog to bite me." She thought, watching him cautiously as she moved closer to the house of interest. The dog didn't move or look threatening. This was a good thing. Running her shaking fingers over her hair, and straightening her dress, she took a deep breath and continued walking.

As Lela approached the fourth house on the left, her eyes scanned the small, unpainted, four-room structure. It had a porch on the front of it and the yard was small and bare. The dirt was packed down so tightly that it was almost shiny, probably due to children playing on it. There were no flowers or shrubbery. It would take a long time for grass to grow there. Separating the yard from the street was a wire fence supported by dark, weathered, locust posts that leaned and were spaced about ten feet apart. There was no gate, only a passage located between two of the posts.

Lela walked through the gateway and stopped very abruptly. She was speechless. There on the porch was a small boy about five or six years old. He was wearing a tee shirt with horizontal blue and white stripes, blue jeans and black and white tennis shoes. His dark blonde hair had been cut neatly in a little boy's style. He was on his knees in "prayer" position with his back to her playing with marbles so intently that he was unaware of Lela's presence. For several minutes, Lela watched him play. "You're so adorable. Could you be my grandson? The thought tempted her to grab him, hold him, squeeze him, and kiss him, but she controlled that urge. It may frighten him.

She could bear it no longer. She stepped up onto the porch and he saw her feet when she placed them down about two feet from him. His eyes focused on her feet and began to move slowly upward. "Mo . . ." His voice stopped before he could finish the word. He leaned back on his feet and took a long look at Lela. "You're not Mommy." He said looking surprised and confused. "You look like Mommy, but you ain't Mommy." He concluded.

"No, I'm not Mommy." Lela assured him as she rubbed her hand across the top of his head as if to pet him. She was still fighting the temptation to grab him. "What's your name? She kindly asked as she stooped to get a better look at him. He had resumed playing with his marbles as if he didn't want her to look at him.

His eyes remained focused on his marbles and he said, "Jimmie."

"Now that's a really good name. I like that name. What's your Mommy's name? Lela asked hoping to hear the word, Maysel.

Looking at her as if to question her sanity and in a tone of frustration, he said, "*Mommy*. Her name's *Mommy*."

Of course it was. How stupid of Lela for not figuring that one out. "Is your Mommy home? She asked.

"Nope." He answered without looking at Lela.

"Do you know where she is? Lela asked

"Yep." Holding onto a marble, he raised his hand in the air and waved his arm back and forth in the direction of the street, he said, "Everybody up and down this street is down at Mary Lou's house." He pointed his finger to a house near the end of the street. "They're peeling and cleanin' peaches. They're gonna put 'em in jars so everybody can eat them later"

"Would you do something for me? She asked.

Jimmie looked at her skeptical and didn't answer.

"Would you go to Mary Lou's house and tell your Mommy that someone would like very much to see her. It's really important. Would you do that for me? She almost pleaded.

"Yes, Ma'am." Jimmie said as he ran from the porch and down the street to deliver Lela's message.

Lela thought she could wait, but the tension made it impossible for her to stay put. She too started walking down the street following Jimmie. He moved much faster than she, but her eyes never left him. Way ahead of her, he made a right turn that took him into Mary Lou's yard. She continued walking slowly. Moments later, a young lady wearing a dress and a very soiled apron appeared and began walking up the street toward Lela. Details of facial features were blocked because of the distance between them and the brightness of the sun. The gap was closing between them. The sun was to Lela's back creating a dark silhouette. No facial features were visible to Maysel because of it. Lela recognized Maysel's body style from her own and began walking a little faster. The two women looked like mirror images. The only difference was that Lela now had a little grey in her hair. Just then, as if angels had adjusted the sunlight with a dimmer switch, the sun dropped behind a cloud and the two women were given a clear view of each other.

"Maysel," Lela whispered. "Maysel." She said a little louder. Her face was wet with tears. Right now, she resented the tears for dimming her vision. Lela could hardly control her emotions. "Maysel. My baby!" She yelled, holding out her arms as she walked.

Maysel thought that she was seeing a ghost and seemed to be in a state of shock and disbelief.

"Mommy? Mommy? Poppy told me you were . . . Mommy is that *really* you? I thought you were d . . ." She couldn't finish any of these statements. Tears stung Maysel's eyes and they overflowed like waterfalls down her face, dripping off her chin. She couldn't believe her eyes. She was actually seeing her mother.

The two finally made contact with a constricting embrace so tight that that neither could breathe. Unable to withstand the emotional force of this reunion, Lela fainted in Maysel's arms as they both sank to the ground in an awesome pool of emotion. Maysel held her mother in her arms and gently rocked her and waited for Lela to revive. At long last, this mother's search was over. She had found her daughter and . . . Her name is Maysel.

About the Author

Johnny McCarty is the third son of Maysel who lived the first 53 years of his life in Southern West Virginia, practicing as a hairdresser for more than 40 of those years. He taught Beauty Culture at the Beckley Institute of Hair Design, and after two years of college, became a pioneer in the Permanent Make-up industry. His dislike for snow prompted him to move south to North Myrtle Beach, SC. He owns and operates Perfect Touch Permanent Make-up Center in Calabash, NC where he practices with physicians and other professionals.

McCarty is a popular guest speaker for national and international organizations and is certified as a Master Instructor through the American Academy of Micropigmentation and the SPCP (Society of Permanent Cosmetic Professionals). He is a Subject Matter Expert in the field and is consulted by practitioners the world over.

He enjoys working, dining with his friends, writing, playing music, impersonating Elvis Presley (professionally) and sharing his life with his beloved pet, Fiona, who is the love of his life. He is excited about writing a sequel to this project and is enjoying putting it all together.

For additonal copies of *My Name is Maysel*, or to schedule a book signing or lecture, contact the author directly at: johnnymccarty@yahoo.com

My Name is Maysel may also be purchased through BarnesandNoble.com and Amazon.com.

My Name is Maysel is now available as a Kindle ebook through Amazon.com

Printed in the United States
220235BV00002B/3/P